PRAISE FOR *LOST ANIMAL CLUB*

"Kevin A. Couture's *Lost Animal Club* is a polished lens that glimpses adolescent mysteries and the lingering puzzles of addiction and sobriety and healing. These haunting stories are populated by bears and bees, cats and dogs, lost animals and lost children and lost parents, evoking a world both charming and stormy, domestic and animal—and it is animal in the best way."
—Mark Anthony Jarman, author of *Knife Party at the Hotel Europa* and *Salvage King, Ya!*

"The stories in *Lost Animal Club* do what the best short fiction excels at: shaping loneliness into art and capturing people in extremis. Kevin A. Couture's sharp, muscular prose gives off emotional jolt after emotional jolt, sparking the reader into thinking about what it means to be human."
—Zsuzsi Gartner, author of *Better Living Through Plastic Explosives*

"Kevin A. Couture's stories are filled with the hurting and the brave, people who seek redemption in whatever ways they can manage. *Lost Animal Club* is a compelling, dexterous collection, full of humanity and insight."
—Julie Paul, author of *The Pull of the Moon*

"These are beautiful stories about survival in social wilderness. I loved them! Read this book. *Lost Animal Club* will find you wherever you are and invite you to come back home."
—Sarah Selecky, author of *This Cake Is for the Party*

LOST ANIMAL CLUB

For Wendy & Eddie,

Thanks for all the support, the love, & the shared up's & down's.

much love

LOST
ANIMAL CLUB
STORIES BY
KEVIN A. COUTURE

NEWEST PRESS
EDMONTON, AB 2016

Library and Archives Canada Cataloguing in Publication

Couture, Kevin A., 1970-, author
Lost animal club / Kevin A. Couture.
(Nunatak first fiction series ; no. 44)
Short stories.
Issued in print and electronic formats.
ISBN 978-1-926455-66-2 (paperback).--ISBN 978-1-926455-67-9 (epub).--
ISBN 978-1-926455-68-6 (mobi)
I. Title. II. Series: Nunatak first fiction ; no. 44
PS8605.O9126L67 2016   C813'.6   C2016-901685-4

Board Editor: Nicole Markotić
Cover design & photography: Kate Hargreaves
Author photograph: David Stewart

Permissions:
SAVE THE LAST DANCE FOR ME
music by **DOC POMUS**
lyrics by **MORT SHUMAN**
© 1960 (Renewed) **UNICHAPPELL MUSIC INC.**
All Rights Reserved

NeWest Press acknowledges the support of the Canada Council for the
Arts, the Alberta Foundation for the Arts, and the Edmonton Arts Council
for support of our publishing program. This project is funded in part by the
Government of Canada.

201, 8540 – 109 Street
Edmonton, AB T6G 1E6
780.432.9427
NeWest Press   www.newestpress.com

No bison were harmed in the making of this book.
PRINTED AND BOUND IN CANADA

CONTENTS

For Maria, Kenzie, and Marlon.

LOST ANIMAL CLUB

"STAY HERE. UNDERSTAND?" I tell my sister. She's scowling at me from the sofa, scrunched up into an annoying little ball.

"You don't have to tell me every time, you know," she says.

I tie my shoes and ignore everything about her.

If we had a TV it wouldn't be so bad leaving her during the day, but we haven't had one for ages. No phone either, no games. Nothing in the kitchen that takes more effort than a can opener and nothing in the closet that isn't broken or meant for babies: a rubber duck with mould around the eyes, a useless pack of diapers, one half of a giant clothespin. Truth is everything we own wouldn't keep a hamster amused for more than five minutes.

"Cezary?" she goes on, "I have questions."

I hold up two fingers.

"Why can't I come with you?"

"You can't keep up. Number two?"

"Can you tell me a joke?"

That was Mom's trick, jokes. The cheapest entertainment around. She'd tell stupid knock-knock stuff to Pillow but I'd get some good ones once in a while. Punch lines she'd have to

9

whisper, starting with, "Don't repeat this to your sister, Cezary. This one's for grownups, okay?"

But Mom's not here anymore. And I have bigger things to worry about.

"No," I say. "There's nothing funny today."

I grab the leash and head to our bathroom, otherwise known as the holding pen. The latest dog—a lab cross with "Dude" written on his tag—lies on the bathmat. He wags his tail as I clip the leash to his collar. Another example of blind trust built on the principle of *what other choice do I have?* The reason this whole thing works.

"Okay, Dude. Time to go."

I lead him to the couch where Pillow's sitting. I usually don't do this but she's had the never-ending wrinkle on her forehead all week. "Take a second," I tell her. "Say goodbye." Her eyes shine as she pets the ridiculous animal, kisses his nose like he was hers all along. I make a *hurry-up* face but let her have this time with him anyway. I can read people the same as animals; the extra few seconds are worth it.

It's a bit of a walk to Dude's house but the dog doesn't mind, exploring bus stops and building corners, investigating mounds of trash along the way. Right now he's looking at me sideways, carrying a Starbucks cup in his mouth like it's free money. Dude's a bit of a moron and all I can hope is this isn't a reflection of his owners. Another hope I'm banking on—that his owners care about him as much as he cares about garbage. When I get close, I take the *Lost Dog* poster out of my pocket. Hold it up like I'm checking the address, like I'm lost myself. It's a good thing too, because there's someone outside patching up the front stairs. A man with a bandana on his forehead, a Raiders shirt, loose jeans with white, powdery stains. He sees me and walks over, pointing with his cement trowel.

"Hey," he says. "That's my dog."

I smile and hold up the poster. "Thank goodness," I say. And though it's over the top, I run with Dude the last little bit, clap my hands when the man takes the leash. I make sure he sees the shirt I'm wearing too, the one with the embroidered hockey skate that makes me look way younger than I actually am. I know from experience—people trust kids a lot more than they trust twelve-year-olds.

"Where did you get him?"

"He was wandering around by the bridge. Lucky I spotted him, I guess."

The man looks into the dog's ears, feels each leg like he's checking for damage. He keeps an eye on me the whole time though, suspicious as a 7-Eleven clerk. "I know what it said on the poster, but there's no reward," he says finally, raising one eyebrow and staring into my face. "I've got nothing for you."

"I'm just happy your dog is safe. That's good enough for me."

I turn and walk down the street, whistle that song from the Lucky Charms commercial, stop and retie my shoelaces.

"Wait," the man yells. He clips Dude to the railing and digs for his wallet. "I was only testing you. Here."

I take the reward and put it in my pocket, doing my best to look surprised instead of desperate. There's no question we need the money way more than he does, but this part—the tense few seconds of contact, the slow-motion handing over of cash—is where I really feel guilty. Where I'm actually embarrassed about this whole friggin' thing.

FROM THE STREET, our apartment building looks abandoned. The weeds, grass, and shrubs are all the colour of weak piss, scorched from the summer heat. Sheets of half-detached stucco flutter in the breeze and the foyer window has a crack I'm sure came from someone's head. To top it off, there's a sign above the door held in place with a rusty coat hanger. *Bella Casa Apartments*. Home.

Inside, I take the stairs to Tem's place.

"You?" Tem says when he answers. The tracksuit he's wearing is so loose you could whip it off him like a magician with a tablecloth. "Why are you at my door?"

"The rent money. My mother sent me over." I hand him the envelope and he counts it four times before stuffing it in his pocket.

"How come she doesn't drop by anymore? I haven't seen her for ages."

"She's working all the time. To pay you."

Tem nods. He seems to like that answer or maybe he can't think of anything else to say. Tem's living proof you don't have to be gifted to be in charge of something. I should be thankful for that I guess. If he was any smarter he might figure out Pillow and I have been living on our own for months and boot us the hell out of there. Or worse, call Social Services.

"Well, say hi to your mother for me," he says. "Tell her I... Just say hi."

"It's a guarantee," I tell him. I nod and head back to the stairs. If I knew where my mother spent her days, though, I'd have a lot more to say to her than, "Hi, from Tem."

When I get to our floor, I take my shoes off and tiptoe down the hallway as softly as I can. It doesn't work; Stan and Lucy, across from us, hear me anyway and storm out of their apartment like a couple of trapdoor spiders. "306," Stan says. He calls me the number on our door.

Stan's a huge man, the kind who has to go through the wheelchair entrance at the ballpark because the turnstiles are too small. His beard is yellow around the mouth from cigarettes and if I had to guess what he did for a living, I'd say a toss-up between pro wrestler and street-corner Santa. Lucy stands behind him, wearing clothes that look homemade but not by someone who actually knows how to make clothes.

"Where's your sweet little sister, Cezary?" she says. "I could just eat her up, you know. Eat her up whole." She makes an exaggerated smacking sound with her lips and I see spit strings stretching across her mouth like elastic bands.

"Inside. With our mother," I say. "I better get in there too, before Mom comes looking."

Stan works his fingers into his beard, then moves off to the side. "Of course," he says. "Go on."

I make a big show of opening all three locks and leave Santa and The Sticky Witch in the hallway, staring giant holes through our cheap wooden door. Even with all those locks, I know they could smash their way through in an instant if they wanted to. Do any manner of horrible things to us before we even had a chance to think about it. Wild and unpredictable as a three-way dogfight.

PILLOW'S ASLEEP ON THE COUCH in the exact spot I left her. She's covered herself with Mom's vinyl raincoat and made a fort with some faded cushions. When Mom left she took all her clothes, (except the raincoat), and most of the blankets with her. She didn't explain but I knew as well as she did: she wasn't coming back anytime soon.

"Cezary?" Pillow says, half asleep. It's the first time she's woken and asked for me instead of Mom. For whatever that's worth.

"What is it?" I say.

"I have questions."

I hold up three fingers.

"Did you find Dude's family?"

"Yes. He's safe at home. They're having a party for him right now."

"Tell me again why you call me Pillow?"

"Because you're soft. Time to sleep."

"*Three*," she says.

I start disassembling her fort.

"When is Mom coming back?"

Mom's never coming back and that's good, we're a lot safer when she's not here. No strange men with dirty hands, no needles on the floor, less chance of a fire. Those are the things to remember about our mother, not the fairy-tale stuff Pillow wants to believe. And if I were smart I'd say that to her right now, right here. Stop her stupid question dead in its stupid tracks.

"Soon, I'll bet," I tell her. "Now go to bed."

"Can I sleep out here instead? It's itchy in there."

"What?"

I lift the makeshift blanket and find red welts up and down her legs, a few of them bleeding where she scratched with her fingernails. I go to the bedroom and pull the sheets back on the mattress. Everything looks normal at first but when I check along the folds, I see them. Tiny bedbugs lining the crevices like spilled salt.

I think about the second-hand quilt I got last month at a garage sale. About the Salvation Army sheets. "Shit," I whisper. "Fuck." I squish a couple of bugs between my fingers and return to the living room. Pillow's conked out again by the time I get there, Mom's coat hanging off her like a melted shield.

"Okay," I whisper, pushing a tuft of hair away from her face. "Tonight we'll both sleep out here on the couch."

"WHAT KIND OF ANIMAL will you rescue today?" Pillow says in the morning. She's still scratching her legs and I have to smack her hand away every thirty seconds.

"I don't know."

"I bet it's a wiener dog. Do you think it's a wiener dog?"

"Let's have a quiet breakfast, okay? No questions."

She slumps in her seat and takes a bite of dry cereal, the scowl on her face intense enough to start a fire. Last night, she kept shifting positions, each time burrowing deeper into my side. Not that I was sleeping anyway but it would have been nice to have the option.

When Mom lived here she'd feed us Rice Krispies in a coffee mug at bedtime, warming the milk to make the cereal taste like caramel. Poor Kid's Pudding, she called it, and I thought it was magic, didn't want anyone to know. But now that I'm older I realize it was just a cheap trick to get us to fall asleep at an appropriate hour. It *was* pretty clever, I have to admit. I'd do the same thing for Pillow too, if we could actually afford to buy milk.

I flick my sister in the arm and tell her to stay out of the bedroom while I'm gone. Before I leave, she stops me.

"Can I make a sign today? For the animals?"

From the look on her face I know it's not worth fighting over. I get a stack of blank sheets from the recycling bin and some stubby old crayons from the drawer. Then I write the words she wants in block letters so she can copy them: LOST ANIMAL CLUB.

I lock the deadbolts behind me when I leave.

After a long walk I start to see fewer broken appliances on the lawns and more underground sprinklers, drivable cars, intact windows with curtains made out of, well, *curtains*. One yard even has a junior swing set off to the side, monkey bars and everything. This means I'm finally fishing in the right waters. Richie Rich territory.

I spy something promising through a chain-link fence across the road—a small, freshly-painted doghouse. When I get to the property line I put my hood up to hide my face and check the street around me. All clear.

I fiddle with the leash in my pocket and make a few smooching noises. Sure enough, a small black nose pokes out of the doghouse. It's a multi-breed thing, smooth, brown, and squat as a baby pig. Not a dachshund like Pillow predicted, but close enough.

"Hey buddy," I whisper. "There's a good boy." He makes his way over and licks my fingers through the metal links. I scratch his chin, look over my shoulder at the empty street. Then I put my hands on the fence and get ready to jump.

"Nelson! Come inside boy. Right now."

A woman on the front steps. Shit, I didn't even hear the door open. She's got a cell phone in one hand, a Milk Bone in the other. The dog trots inside the house and the woman starts dialling her phone.

I push the leash deep in my pocket. Keep my face hidden behind my hood.

"I just wanted to pet your nice dog. I thought he could be my friend," I say, slurring the words a little like that kid from second grade with Down Syndrome. "Oh boy, I guess I should have asked permission first. That's what they tell me at the group. *Always ask permission.* But sometimes I forget things."

She stares at me curiously, puts her phone away. And I know I've got her.

But just to finish things off I crouch down, wrap my hands around my knees, and rock back and forth on the sidewalk. Then I jump up and scream, "I'm so stupid sometimes!" and I run, flailing my arms in all directions like I'm being attacked by something. By insects, by nature. A million invisible shocks in the air all around me.

ON THE WAY HOME I STOP at the drugstore to try and salvage the wasted day. It's a seedy place with a gang of homeless men outside passing smokes back and forth. One of them has dried blood on his face, brown lines running from his nostrils like slug trails. He yells something when I approach but it turns into a long, wet coughing fit. I slip by him into the store.

The pharmacist, a small man with a lab coat and an English accent, gives me a pesticide specifically for bedbugs, *Suspend*. I also get a pack of heavy-duty garbage bags, some Saran Wrap, a stack of quarters for the laundromat. And on a whim, I splurge for a chocolate bar for Pillow to keep her from being a pain in the ass tonight.

As I'm paying I think about the drugs behind the pharmacist's counter. I remember being here once with Mom, early on, as she tried to get a prescription filled. They denied it and Mom yelled at the pharmacist, a different man than the one here today. He shrugged and told her, "Maybe you should go to the hospital, to Emergency if you're in pain."

"The hospital?" she laughed. "Oh, they get you started all right. The first one's always free, isn't that right, Cezary?"

I didn't know how to answer that and I didn't really know what she meant. The only times I could think of when Mom had been to the hospital were when Pillow was born and, presumably, me. I can only guess what kind of drugs they give you for that.

Outside, the smoking men have joined another group. One of them has a pit bull with a thick studded collar, no leash. The dog barks and slug-nose gives me the finger as I come out; I go the long way into an extended alley between two tenements.

There's a muggy, shit-faced man halfway down the lane, slumped against a blue dumpster. When I walk past, he says, "Hey. What's in the bag?" I ignore him even though he repeats it over and over. I'm almost at the end of the alley when I hear another noise. Somebody moaning from the bottom of a basement stairwell. I want to look even though it's none of my business, even though it's the wrong thing to do. I clutch the drugstore bag to my chest and walk towards the railing.

A man and a woman are lying in the filth at the bottom of the stairs, their belongings spread around them like this is their home. The man's naked, covered in washed-out tattoos and the woman's so thin I can count backbones through the fabric of her t-shirt. There's something black—vomit, maybe—crusted into the woman's hair and both of them have rubber tubes coiled around their arms like thick bands of ivy. The smell of burning plastic, everywhere. I'm about to leave when the woman moans and rolls over on the cement. I feel blood, dark and cold, racing through the veins in my eyes.

My mother. Right there below me, not six feet away.

I don't know whether to throw up or scream. It isn't supposed to happen like this, finding her on the street. I'd only ever considered two options before. One, she comes back for good; or two, we never see her again. But this? What am I supposed to do with this? I clutch the railing and squeeze until the metal cuts into my fingers.

Then my mother sits up. She squints, turns her head. I jump back before she can recognize me.

"Hey! I asked you what's in that fucking bag!" the dumpster man says. He's right behind me now, reaching for the pharmacy stuff. He's slow but manages to close his fingers on the bag anyway, yanking it towards him. It tears when I pull it back and I wrap my arms around the loose contents. I leave him by the stairs and run down the alley, faster than an electric shock, faster than an argument. Faster than a blindside punch.

PILLOW'S DECORATED OUR PLACE with ten or eleven signs, all saying the same thing: *Lost Animal Club.* She jumps up and down as she shows me, tapping the letters and telling me her versions of the colours she used. "Squirrel-brown. Cat-paw. Turtle-tongue. Nose." I follow her because I have to, but when I look at the signs and the chunky block-lettering all I see is the scene at the bottom of a filthy stairwell, Mom's face turning towards me, the waste all around her. Her eyes. Her eyes. Her eyes.

"Cezary! Pay attention," Pillow says, tugging my sleeve.

She drags me on, continuing the tour until we've seen them all. And when she's done, I fix her up with some dry crackers and salt—the only thing we have because I lost the chocolate bar in the alley—and I get to work on the bedroom. Nobody else is going to do it. If I didn't know that before, I sure as hell do now.

I borrow a vacuum from Tem and use it to suck up the bedbugs, dumping them in the trash outside. I seal the blankets into plastic bags and take what's left of the food money from beneath the mattress—the same place Mom used to hide it— and put it safely in my pocket. Then I lift the bed on its side; it slips and I bang my shin on the box spring, sweat dripping off the tip of my nose. Finally, I lean it against the wall and coat the entire place with *Suspend.* The corners of the room, both sides of the mattress, the doorframe, the back of the closet. When I'm done, I cover the bed in Saran Wrap and flop it into place on the box spring. The powder in the room rises up and settles back on the floor, slowly, like something sinking to the bottom of a deep, deep lake.

I curl up on the plastic-covered mattress and before I know it, tears start pooling on the Saran Wrap under my eyes. It's stupid, but I can't shut it down. When the crying finally runs its course, I dry my face with the pesticide-free part of my hand.

"Cezary?" Pillow says, standing in the doorway. She's making that face again. I get up and walk out of the bedroom with her, closing the door behind us.

"Let me guess," I say. "Questions?"

"Uh huh."

I flash three fingers at her.

"What are you thinking about?"

"Roses and ladybugs."

"Do you have any jokes today?"

"No. Still nothing funny. Final question?"

"Will I go to school this year?"

School? I hadn't thought about that. Truth is, neither one of us is likely to go to school ever again.

"We'll see," I say, turning away.

There's a knock on the door before she can bring up anything else. It's Tem, his eyes darting around the whole apartment. "Time's up," he says. "I'm here for my vacuum."

He checks out Pillow's stupid signs while I bring the machine in from the other room.

"Where's your mother now? Is she working again? On Sunday?"

"No, she's here. Sleeping, though, sick as a dog."

"Is that right?" Tem stares at the closed bedroom door.

"What kind of sick?"

I lower my head like I'm about to let him in on a secret. "Pillow, come here. But don't get too close." I pull her pant leg up to reveal the red bumps.

"What's that?"

Pillow opens her mouth to say something; I cover it with my hand. "Have you ever had the chicken pox?" I ask Tem.

"I'm not sure."

"You'd better be sure. If you get them now, at your age, it's terrible."

"Yeah. I think I've heard about that. Shingles, right?"

"Exactly," I say, though I have no idea what he means.

He points to the bedroom door. I hand him his vacuum.

"I hope she gets better soon. Tell her I said that, okay?"

"It's a guarantee," I tell him.

He heads down the hallway holding the vacuum away from him like it's a bag of diapers. I start to think maybe there *is* a way to fool the school board so Pillow can go to Kindergarten after all. We could slip her in the back door, fake the paperwork, fill out the forms ourselves. I'm getting pretty good at Mom's signature these days and as long as Pillow keeps her mouth shut...

Suddenly the door across the hall opens and Stan appears, rocking back and forth, stony-faced, silent as the plague. The reject must've been watching from his peephole the whole time. He scratches his bare stomach, rubs the stretch marks on his skin. Stares right past me into the apartment where Pillow's standing, still showing off her spotted leg.

I DON'T SEE A SINGLE PERSON on the street the next morning. Usually I like it quiet but today I wish for a building fire or a carnival, a street-fight. Any distraction that doesn't involve me directly.

As I walk, I think about our mother. I wonder—now that I know where she is—if I should go back and check on her. I'm not saying she should *come home* or anything, but maybe I could visit her once in a while to make sure she's okay. Bring a sandwich or some toothpaste, a care package like you do for someone in prison. And later, if all went well, Pillow might come along too. If we knew when Mom was getting high we could work around it, schedule some appointments. Write everything down on a calendar.

I stop in front of an abandoned coffee shop. The walls inside have been tagged with graffiti and someone's set up a broken toilet in the corner, dark stains and ripped newspaper all over it. There are wine bottles and grocery bags on the floor, remnants of a campfire. I try to look at my reflection in the window but the leftover pieces of unbroken glass are too small. In my mind, for some reason, I picture our apartment back home.

What kind of idiot am I? The idea to visit Mom is about as dumb as punching yourself in the mouth to find out if there really is a tooth fairy. I can't afford to think that way and I know what I need to do. Forget about Mom and focus on taking care of Pillow. The family member who didn't disappear. The one who stayed.

I head back the same way as yesterday, back to Nelson's yard. When I get there, I sneak up to the far side of the house, out of sight of the front door. I give a whistle and Nelson wags his tail which makes this decision easy. He scampers over like this whole thing is his idea, buzzing at the fence line, spinning in circles. The trust in his eyes burning brighter than the morning sun.

NELSON WEAVES BACK AND FORTH in the hallway, sniffing the disgusting carpet, licking up crumbs of who-knows-what. He's quiet though, thank God, and we get all the way to our door without a bark. I hold his collar tight as I duck below the neighbours' peephole. Then I reach up, put the key in the first lock, and give it a turn.

It's already unlocked.

"Pillow?" I whisper. I walk inside and drop Nelson's leash. He scurries off and disappears into the bathroom.

The apartment is never pristine but right now it looks worse than ever, I'd even say *rummaged*. Overturned cushions, crayons on the floor, drawers open. I'm about to call out again when I hear a noise from the bedroom. The thump of the mattress and the box spring scraping against the floor—something Pillow's too small to do on her own.

I grab a knife from the kitchen counter. And my hand, my whole body, starts to shake as the bedroom door opens.

"Cezary, baby!"

Mom. Right here in the apartment. Up close she looks even worse than she did in the stairwell. Her skin's pale and sweaty and there are needle marks up and down her arm like dead stars. She's shoeless and her toenails are a sickly yellow colour, her feet dusted with bug powder from the bedroom floor.

But she came back. That means something, doesn't it?

Pillow's standing inside the bedroom and I relax my hand, bring the knife down to my side.

"What are you doing here?" I ask Mom.

"What am I doing? Sweetheart, I've missed you guys and I want to make it up to you. For everything."

For a second I picture Mom living at home again. Making dinners. Washing sheets. Answering Pillow's dumb questions. But that dream gets swamped by the image of her lying face down in a disgusting stairwell.

"Where have you been all this time?"

"Missing you, that's where."

"Yes, but where *exactly?*"

Pillow comes out of the bedroom and Mom grabs her, pulls her in.

"You haven't changed at all, Cezary," Mom says, waving her hand in my direction like she's clearing fruit flies. "You know, I dreamed I saw you the other day. It felt so real, like you were right there. But before I knew it, *poof.*"

I shouldn't be ashamed of how I reacted in the alley but the back of my neck burns just the same. "Pillow, why don't you come over here?" I say.

"Oh, she's fine. We've been having a ball, telling all sorts of jokes. Haven't we, my love?"

Pillow nods, but she has lines on her cheeks where fresh tears have washed away the dust.

"I've got some new jokes for you too, Cezary," Mom continues. "Want to hear one?"

"I don't know."

"Well, I ran into Tem on the way in. He asked if I was

21

feeling better. That's funny, right?"

I blink, but say nothing.

"He thanked me for being regular with the rent these days, too. Also funny, since I haven't been paying him. The whole thing got me wondering, where would Cezary get the money for that? Did you have a windfall I don't know about, sweetie? You can tell me."

The food money in my pocket suddenly feels as obvious as a missing eye. I open my mouth but before I can answer, Pillow starts sobbing. "We. Got. It. From. The. Animals," she says in short, pathetic gasps. "Cezary. Rescues. Them."

Mom has no idea what Pillow's talking about and she's getting antsy. Drumming her fingers on Pillow's collarbone. "That's a good one, I guess," she says. "But the real question here is where you stashed—"

"306?" a voice asks, cutting her off. It's Stan, calling out from the doorway. He stands there breathing heavily through his nose, flanking me between Mom and himself.

Lucy rushes in behind him holding an ancient phone in her hand, the long cord stretching over to their apartment. "What's going on here?" she says. "What's happening?"

No one answers, the whole room has gone deep-lake silent. Then Stan walks slowly towards Pillow and my mother. His hands clenched, his upper body vibrating. The muscles in his jaw as tight as Doberman's.

"Cezary, cut him!" Mom yells, squeezing Pillow's arm.

I lift the knife without thinking.

"Yes, stab him. *Now!*" Mom goes on.

I don't move and Stan walks right past me, stopping in front of my mother. Her face changes, reminding me of those men beside the pharmacy. Stan grabs Pillow, pulls her away, and lifts her to his chest. I'm still pointing the knife at him. But what now?

"You can save her, Cezary. Do it for us." Mom's voice is soft now and the tone she's using makes it sound like if I did this, Pillow and I would be safe again. Everything back to normal. I lift the knife higher.

Pillow's fingers clutch Stan's shirt. She's not trying to escape though and I don't know how to strike without hurting her. I want to yell, *Run away, Pillow. Hit back, do something.* But then she puts her head against Stan's shoulder, wraps her arms further around him. And I think I understand.

Blind trust.

I drop the knife to the floor, kick it so it slides underneath the couch. Immediately, Stan puts my sister down in front of me and tells her to take my hand.

"You fuck-ups," Mom yells. She rushes over and reaches under the couch for the blade. The rest of the room comes to life.

Nelson the idiot dog emerges, barking like he's on fire. Stan corners Mom against the far wall. Lucy punches buttons on her phone as though she's calling in an air strike. Everybody's yelling, screaming at everybody else, oblivious to my sister and me right there in the middle of it all.

"Come on," I whisper, tugging Pillow's sleeve. Her skin is frighteningly pale except for the crimson bug-bites dotting her arms. "We have to go," I say, louder this time. I drag her backwards until we get to the open door. Nobody notices us. We're almost free.

At the entrance to the hallway, Pillow stops. "Wait," she says. She shakes me off and runs back into the apartment, straight towards our mother.

"No, Pillow. Don't!" I say. I try to follow but get caught up in Lucy's phone cord, Nelson nipping at my feet. "She's not the same person..."

But Pillow doesn't stop at our mom. Instead, she runs past her to the other side of the room. She reaches up, grabs one of her new, colourful signs, and tears it off the wall.

Lucy waves her phone in the air, Mom punches Stan's shoulder, and Stan yells at her, loud and deep and menacing. Pillow ignores it all, racing from wall to wall taking down the posters like balloons at the end of a party. Every last one of them. When she's done, she runs back, clutching them to her chest with one arm.

Everybody stops fighting; I grab Pillow's sleeve and we run into the corridor.

We rush down the stairs and slam the fire door behind us.

I don't hear anyone chasing, but we keep moving just in case. In the lobby, I wrap my hoodie around my sister to protect her from the elements, to stop her from looking back. She isn't though, not even when we get outside and the summer rain starts to fall. The heat from the pavement turning water into steam beneath our feet.

THE RABBIT

THE LOBBY'S TANGLED WITH MARATHONERS, a giant game of pick-up sticks. Tourist-runners mostly, looking for a photo op or directions to the souvenir table, a place to dump their luggage. Sue recognizes a few elites in the crowd, all businesslike as they sidestep the hotel's many distractions, but hopes none of them notice her. The drone of a thousand suitcase wheels is giving her a headache, making her teeth itch. And her veins feel like they're set to explode from the unnatural buildup of tension that always permeates these events. How could anyone in their right mind come here looking for a good time?

Sue's husband is across the room at the reception desk. The woman he's talking to is attractive, no question about it, but she isn't Trent's type. Sue can't help but notice the excess flesh on her neck and shoulders hiding all her delicate bones like a bathrobe; she imagines the margarine softness of her butt, her stomach, the bulk of her inner thighs. No, it isn't the receptionist Sue has to worry about. It's the others—the fit, young runners with negative body fat and impossibly tiny frames—who're unfurling Sue's insecurities. All of them so slight they could use a man's belt as a hammock. Trent's belt for example.

"You are the rabbit," someone says. "I remember you from last year."

"Yes."

Chebichi, the only Kenyan in the women's field. Her eyes are like coconut water and her skin, smooth and taut as cherries. In the same marathon a year ago Chebichi came fifth behind Eri Shinohara from Tokyo, Ashley Bachman from California, and the two Russians, Tatiana and Denisova. She has far more ambition than Sue ever had for running. Not that Sue's a quitter, anything but. She just doesn't have that same internal drive to achieve, well, *excellence.*

"Your pace last year was quite good for me," Chebichi goes on. "This time I can do better, I think. You see what I mean?"

"I'll do my best."

Chebichi pats her back. "Yes," she says. "But now I must settle in my room." She walks off and disappears up a staircase.

Sue's not sure if she should be angry or flattered. Threatened, maybe, is a better word. Chebichi's beautiful and she's one of the tiniest runners Sue has ever known.

She retreats against a wall under a painting of a traditional Hawai'ian catamaran, one of dozens gracing the hotel foyer. The tables around her boast illuminated mini-fountains and thick crystal vases with orchids as bright as parrots. There's a bowl of fruit at every entrance spilling over with mangoes and bananas, whole pineapples as big as a meal. The entire place arranged to resemble paradise. And it would be too if only she and Trent were here alone, on holiday. Madly in love.

The receptionist hands Trent two key cards and points to the elevators at the far end of the room. He touches her arm, sniffs the flowers beside him. Even from here, from her limited view, Sue can tell he's winking. He strolls over to join her in front of the painting.

"Fourth floor," he says. "I upgraded."

HOW THEY ENDED UP IN HONOLULU again is a bit of a blur. Trent wanted to go, yes, but Sue didn't. There are plenty of other races in cities where women wear clothes instead of bikinis. But by the time she worked out a useable excuse he'd already booked the flight, arranged a hotel, and called the marathon office on her behalf. Hard to argue his point though, the trip's better than free when you factor in the payment Sue gets for pacesetting. And it's guaranteed money, something no other runner here can claim.

"Hotels never change, do they?" Trent says. "TV, dresser, big ugly lamp." He pats each item as he speaks as if they were small dogs or children's heads. Then he falls back on the bed and bounces, stretching his arms out. "King size is cool though. Big enough for you and three more. A quartet of runners."

Sue unwraps the soap and washes travel-film from her face. The tangles in her hair pinch when she runs a brush through.

Trent's not a runner himself but he enjoys the company of athletes. Thin, tight-bodied athletes. It's what first attracted him to Sue four years ago at the *Harry Jerome Track Meet* in Vancouver. Back then she was the skinniest on the field and during the five km event, he watched her drop out at 3000 m. At the after-party he came right up to her as though they were intimate already, a trait that made her feel much less an outcast.

"Why did you bail?" he asked. "You were easily the fastest."

"I'm the pacesetter. It's my duty." Then she waited for the inevitable questions, all-knowing and judgmental as an owl: *You never finish? Ever? How does that make you feel?*

But instead, he *complimented* her. "Job well done, then. The competitors ran a terrific race and you deserve a victory hug." He lifted her right off the ground making her squeal and dig her fingers into the thick muscles of his back. When he finally put her down, he smiled as if he'd just figured out a Chinese puzzle box. Fast forward a year, he asked her to marry him and just like that they were committed. Signed up. No forfeiting allowed.

Trent scratches his chin and bounces off the bed. "I'll get the tickets for tonight before they sell out," he says, giving Sue an exaggerated salute from the door. "You wait here."

SUE UNPACKS HER SUITCASE and hangs up her outfit for later, a blue strapless bubble dress bought especially for the trip. Considering the sexy, athletic crowd she'll encounter at the luau, it's the absolute least she can do. There's a can of Pringles and some chocolate macadamias in the minibar but she goes instead for the six-dollar bottle of flavoured, vitamin water; she's up two pounds this year already. The water, despite how good it's supposed to be, sticks in her throat like road dust. Makes her crave something as outrageous as an ice cream float.

When Sue was young, everyone had high hopes for her *natural ability*. Her parents came to all her races, drove to the early morning practices. They stopped buying bacon and ice cream and instead stocked up on boneless-skinless chicken breasts, protein bars, big bags of prewashed spinach. But when her coach—somewhere around Grade Nine—spoke of Junior World Championships and Olympic contention, Sue began governing herself. Holding back just enough to blend in. To remain, respectably, in the front section of the B crowd where she belonged. Now with Trent in the picture, a huge mortgage, bills, commitments, that's as far as she'll ever go. Most days she's fine with that idea. In fact, she hardly ever thinks about what it would be like to break through that ribbon anymore.

She *is* the best pacesetter out there, no one argues that. She runs a steel-tough standard, her cadence as smooth as a greyhound's. Race organizers love her and in the last three competitions she's been in, she was the only one they even considered.

So why does she feel so unappreciated?

In the courtyard below her window: rows of red-cushioned lounge chairs bordered by stoic palms, a grass roof hut serving as a bar for the massive hotel pool already full of bodies in brightly coloured swimsuits. A sign on the hut says, *Welcome Marathoners!* It's where the tickets for the luau are being sold. Trent, however, is nowhere in sight.

He's never cheated on her. Never. Trent's a flirt, yes. A man who loves women, yes. But he's not—*not*—a cheat.

Sue needs to let go of the little things. The way he touches elbows and kisses hands when he meets her friends. How he wants to have sex after watching women's tennis. How he leaves his ring at home when he bartends to get better tips. None of this is bad, not even when Sue adds it all up. But these details gnaw at her like sand fleas at her ankles. Knocking her—ever so slightly—off her game.

Before the marathon last year, Trent told her, "It's heaven, Sue. Honestly. When you die, this is where you go." They were walking Kuhio Beach and she hoped he meant the gorgeous manako trees, the smell of exotic flowers, their walking hand in hand. But the farther they went, the more she worried he was referring to something else—the women on the beach around them. Half naked, sun-warmed, lying on the sand like lost coins. Later, the day after the race, Trent disappeared for hours and his only explanation was, "I'm manufactured to wander around sometimes. That's just me, honeybee."

That time, Sue had very nearly confronted him. She was that close.

The door opens and Trent strolls in holding two luau tickets. "Got 'em," he says, a bead of sweat rolling down the side of his face. He throws the tickets on the table, heads directly into the washroom and starts up the shower.

Sue wants to ask, *hey, what took so long?* Instead, she leans against the door and says, "Good job, honey." Then she grabs the bag of macadamias, sits on the bed, and waits quietly for him to finish.

TRENT TAKES AN EXTRA-LONG TIME in the shower which makes Sue want to pace the room. As though he's in there with someone else or at least the fantasy of someone else. She's being stupid again, she knows. It's because they just arrived and she needs a little while to acclimatize. That's how it is at these races, how it's always been even before Trent came along. And this feeling isn't exactly something she can talk about, not with him. That'd be like bathing in pollen to try and treat your allergies.

Trent opens the bathroom door and fog billows out into the room. There's the scent of spearmint and pine, his favourite shampoo, in the warmth of the steam cloud. Sue puts the rest of the macadamias away and listens to him whistle a song, tapping the beat on the shell-covered countertop. It bothers her he's so cheery. That he can sing while she sits and clenches the muscles in her toes, the soles of her feet. Picks the skin around her thumbnail until it throbs.

"How's my little speed queen?" Trent says, leaning against the doorframe. He walks over to the bed wearing only the smallest of hotel towels. There's a bulge in front and Sue has to decide whether to ignore it or get in the mood. He runs his hand through her hair, squeezes her neck, kisses her shoulder. His skin, still hot from the shower.

She closes her eyes and sees Trent down by the pool, getting all turned on by the sunbathers, the thin, wet bodies of other runners. She tries to return his kisses but right now she feels about as sexy as a stick of beef jerky.

He moves his hand down her body. Sue stops him at the buttons. "Maybe later?" she asks.

He's trying, Sue can tell, to hide his disappointment. "That's okay," he tells her. "You've probably got the big race on your mind." He kisses her forehead and returns to the bathroom, no longer whistling anything at all.

THE LUAU'S UNDER A SERIES of huge white canopies with torches in tall stands around the perimeter. Down in front, past all the rows of tables, sits an ornate, peach-coloured band shell with a podium for the evening's host—a race coordinator named Jack who looks a lot like Kenny Rogers. He roams around on the glittering stage with a microphone, thanking sponsors and telling lousy jokes about hitting the wall. People laugh because they're in paradise and it's okay to make concessions. Okay to make a fool of yourself.

There are more men here than women but what concerns Sue are the tenacious groups of single women in their clingy outfits and natural tans, on the lookout for a Hawai'ian tryst. It's a minefield of temptation just to get to the buffet table and right now Sue regrets not having sex with Trent this afternoon. What the hell was she thinking?

"Not hungry?" he says. He points to Sue's plate with his fork. She took only a bite of pineapple, some Caesar salad, and a slice of Lomi Lomi salmon no bigger than a candy bar.

"I'm pacing myself," she says, but Trent doesn't get it.

He's preoccupied with the women next to him, runners from Nagoya who, unfortunately, speak perfect English. One of them, Michiko wearing a strapless cocktail dress no bigger than a pillowcase, leans into him when she speaks. Her hair's tied back in a ponytail and as she turns to giggle with her friend, it brushes against Trent's shoulder.

The staff brings out more food while a group of entertainers take the stage. Shirtless men with tattoos and necklaces made of long shells; women in grass skirts and coconut bikini tops shaking Polynesian maracas. They begin the performance and Trent whispers something to Michiko that makes her cover her mouth and laugh. He's being friendly. Pointing out how the performers' hips, as dense as bread dough, are designed for Hula dancing not running. Or maybe he's making fun of the host—Jack/Kenny in his buttermilk suit jacket. The kind of *laugh-but-don't-get-caught-laughing* comedy routine Trent does when he's in a crowd. The difference here is it should be *her* at the end of his whispering lips, not Michiko. If Sue were a different kind of person she'd run her fingers through Trent's hair, straddle his lap and kiss him passionately right here, right now, right in front of everyone.

"Hello again my friend."

Chebichi, standing behind her.

"Hello," Sue replies.

"Good choice with the salmon. Carbohydrate loading is a myth." Chebichi touches the edge of Sue's plate with her elegant fingers. Her lower back and stomach are exposed, the muscles firm and smooth as baby turtles. Trent's eyes wander all over her.

"Hello there." He takes Chebichi's hand and gently kisses her wrist. "I'm Trent."

"You must be the husband. Hello." Chebichi slides in between them, sandwiching Trent between herself and Michiko. "Have you decided on your exit point?" she asks.

At first, Sue's not sure if she's still talking to Trent or to her. "No, not yet," she answers.

Trent's head moves up and down, almost imperceptibly, as he takes in Chebichi's bare skin. He turns to Michiko and whispers something in her ear; she shakes her head and slaps his arm. The only thing missing is for a stark naked runner to fall from the sky, land in Trent's lap and start wiggling.

"Just trying to orient myself," Chebichi goes on.

"I haven't figured it out yet."

"You should. To give you focus."

The performance ends and Trent applauds. Then he rests his arm on the back of Michiko's chair, grazing her hair with his fingers in the process. At least he's still wearing his wedding ring, that's one good thing.

Sue closes her eyes. Of course he's wearing his ring. What's wrong with her?

Chebichi pokes Sue's elbow and says, "The halfway point, I believe, is the community of Waialae Iki. Will you do half?"

"Look. I really, really don't know. Okay?" Sue answers, louder and harsher than she intended. The blood in her face feels thick as lava and her heart strains to milk it through her rapidly-burning arteries.

Chebichi wrinkles her forehead. She turns to Trent and Michiko, huddling together, laughing. Then she leans towards Sue to whisper. "It's of no consequence if he does not wish to be stolen," she says. "How can you expect to run your own race if you keep looking over your shoulder at his?"

SUE GETS UP FIRST. Trent, still wrapped in the bed sheet, will hibernate a while yet. Despite wanting to turn in early, she and Trent closed down the luau last night. And true to form, he disappeared for almost an hour, leaving her alone at the table. Also true to form, he came back to her. He doesn't want to be stolen. He doesn't want to be stolen. He doesn't want to be stolen.

But if she continues being so jealous, will he?

She decides to do an easy run along the race route to clear her head.

The actual starting point for the marathon is along Ala Moana Boulevard but Sue takes a cab to mile five, Waikiki Beach, and starts from there. There are high-rise condos on her left, and on her right, the vast expanse of sand and surf. She pauses at a busy crossing where the waves roll hypnotically in the distance and surfers fight to find a spot in the cresting water.

The pathway around the beach is equally crowded: joggers, rollerbladers, a man and woman strolling hand in hand. Blissful.

A group of tourists have gathered around the statue of Duke Kahanamoku and his surfboard. Two young girls step forward and touch the statue's bronze muscles while their friend takes a picture. Sue remembers this monument from last year, remembers the biography she read of Duke's life. Olympic athlete, surfer, police officer, playboy. When he finally settled down, was his wife jealous too? By all accounts, Duke flirted terribly. But then again, by all accounts, they somehow had a wonderful marriage. It's not the same situation as Sue's of course, but close enough to make her wonder, *What was their secret?*

The light turns and Sue runs on. Soon, she's climbing the hill circling Diamond Head Crater. It's fairly steep and she feels it in her legs, a nice burn, as if her muscles are massaging themselves. Working out her stress. For a while she thinks only of the sensation in her thighs, the flow of blood, how she'll run tomorrow. The pace.

From the top of the crater, she sees a good section of the course along Oahu's coastline and the development communities below. Also where the course doubles back, heading into Kapiolani Park, the finish line, where everyone will strive to be tomorrow. Past that, somewhere in the city proper, lies Trent, alone in their hotel room. Still sleeping as if there are no worries in the world. As if they're in paradise.

Sue stops running and rests with her hands on her knees. The vista before her, the warm morning sun.

They *are* in paradise.

Chebichi's right, Sue's spent so much time alone at the front of the pack she's become paranoid of what's been happening behind her. But it shouldn't matter. A marriage, like a race, depends on the effort of the participants, the way they push each other to do better. The only control she has is over her own performance and it should always, *always* be her best effort. If she does that, logically, Trent will do the same. A pace they can both handle.

She turns around and runs back towards Honolulu. Back towards her husband.

Sᴜᴇ's sᴡᴇᴀᴛʏ ᴀɴᴅ ᴛɪʀᴇᴅ when she reaches the hotel, but feels better than she has in a long time. A few people mill about the half-empty lobby but nobody she recognizes; elites all train at this hour. She takes the stairs up to their floor to get one final burn in her legs, the blood flowing to her groin, transferring her body heat to the right places. When she's ready, she takes a deep breath and opens the door to their room.

The bed is empty.

She steadies herself against the wall. But then she hears the shower—Trent is just in the shower—which is even better than perfect.

Sue strips and washes her body at the sink with a face-cloth, puts on a skimpy pair of panties and nothing else. And she jumps into bed to wait for Trent, her running partner, to finish. She's excited, energized like at the start of a race. She'd forgotten the difference between that kind of excitement and her usual anxiety. It's the same feeling she used to get when she ran competitively, when she challenged herself. When she actually had something on the line.

Their clothes from last night are on the floor beside the bed. Sue gets up and throws them over a chair to clear the route. Some change falls out of Trent's pocket and rolls off under the table. Something else falls out too.

A crumpled up, empty condom wrapper.

The shower stops. Sue picks up the wrapper. Trent comes out of the washroom with a towel around his waist.

"Hey," he says. "You're back."

Sᴜᴇ's ᴏɴᴇ ᴏꜰ ᴛʜᴇ ꜰɪʀsᴛ ᴛᴏ ᴀʀʀɪᴠᴇ, along with Chebichi. The park around them slowly fills with expectant runners, at first in ones and twos, then big groups. The scene resembling a massive human wedge—the pack getting larger and denser the farther back one goes from the starting line. All these people, undoubtedly, live much better lives than Sue.

A voice over the ᴘᴀ system tells everyone to get set. Building tension for the tourists. The voice mentions the fans, congratulating them for getting up so early to support their family members and friends. A cheer rises from the observers' section off to the left. Sue doesn't flinch. Trent might be there, he might not. She joins the elites at the front of the line.

The Russians take turns lying on the grass, stretching each other's legs over their heads, focused as two sparrow-hawks. Ashley Bachman stands beside them. She's in great shape, another to watch. It's a deep field so there's really no telling who the winner will be.

Just before the scheduled starting pistol, Chebichi joins Sue at the front. She's fidgeting, twisting side to side, distracted. "Hey rabbit," she says, jogging on the spot beside her. "You never did say at what point you'll drop out."

Sue tilts her head to the side to crack the joint in her shoulder. "I know," she says, scanning the mob behind her, brisk and young and full of promise. Then she channels her energy, faces the road ahead. Gets herself into position.

LEMONADE FREE

THERE'S A KID WITH A LEMONADE STAND down the block from the meeting house. Porcelain sugar bowl, fancy toothpick umbrellas, lime circles straddling the plastic cups—a fairly slick operation. He sits in one of those lawn chairs that fold into a long sack like a rifle case, sipping on a cold one himself, grinning like a leprechaun with his purple bag of coins on his washed-out plastic table. Way more than I can handle, I walk around the opposite way.

We meet at Joey's place, no reason except his basement is large enough. Joey lives on a quiet street and everybody likes it quiet, especially the newbies. Joey's is exactly two-and-a-quarter miles from the nearest drink, Pokanos Bar and Grill. A little joint with dim lighting, stuffed deer heads on the walls, a big set of moose antlers. The bartender's a guy named Domingo who sports a strawberry wraparound goatee and wears black t-shirts too small in the arms. I know the bus route to Pokanos off by heart. Everyone else does too, whether they admit it or not.

Truth is I avoid the bus these days, that route in particular, and I don't drive although I still have my licence. My wife—my *ex-wife*—Crystal, told me over and over not to drive under the influence. Not to drive in an altered state of mind. "Sooner or later, Lewis," she warned. "Sooner. Or. Later."

But that was a lifetime ago. As of noon today, I've been sober exactly one year and the group is hosting a party in honour of my not fucking it all up. We're a small group so besides Joey, who's been dry a decade, no one's reached twelve months without a slip. And it's unfortunate but everybody, all of them, will be there today. A genuine red letter bash, an AA barn-burner. Coffee and cigarettes in shaky hands, iced tea and juice, cake with a big number twelve or *Way to Go!* on it. They'll slap me on the back and nod their heads. Firefly energy all over the room 'cause everyone associates a party with getting bombed. Someone's bound to sneak away early and catch the express bus to Pokanos. Happens every time we meet.

IF A PERSON COULD GO BACK IN TIME, would outcomes change? Or is everything set and we just bounce around inside some giant, cosmic Mason jar, our lives determined by the guy who pokes holes in the lid for air? I chew on this quite often during my walk to Joey's and today, because it's an anniversary, I'm brooding more than ever. Nothing like a milestone to make you exhume your choices, sift through the wreckage, pull out a magnifying glass. Backtrack.

Everyone in the group evaluates their mistakes, not just me. Memories of plastic cup kegger-nights, beer funnel parties, washroom-floor mornings with bathmat fibres imprinted on our grey, flattened cheeks. Phil, the Group Service Rep, told us when he was fourteen he downed a two-six of Crown Royal from his dad's liquor cabinet. Phil got so messed up he put his sister's dachshund in the microwave just like that urban legend. Or who knows, maybe Phil started the damn thing. He ran around the kitchen swatting his sister with a bag of buns yelling, "Hotdogs! Who wants hotdogs?" Later, unable to register what he'd done, Phil told his sister, "But I only had it on defrost." His face folded in on itself when he told us that story, his eyebrows dragging his forehead down like rakes. Hard to imagine Phil was ever fourteen.

Then there's me, telling the story of Crystal and my first date. Hallowe'en, Scare-aoke night at the Cranberry Arms. Crystal dressed up as Cleopatra complete with beaded head-piece and golden armbands, and sang *Killer Queen*. She sounded great and looked even better, though I didn't join her performance. Too busy getting sozzled. Back then my drinking had a certain charm, a mischievous quality like a young Dean Martin. Crystal doesn't know this but a block after I dropped her off I passed out behind the wheel of my tangerine Sunfire. Puked all over myself. Couldn't get the smell out of the car for weeks and had to fork out fifty for the trashed, rented Robin Hood costume.

Eight years, Crystal and I. How she lasted that long I'll never know. When we had our daughter, Kimberly, I did stop drinking for a while. I couldn't enjoy a beer anymore with Kimberly's amethyst eyes blinking. Her little harmonica cries as she searched for Crystal's breast, fingers grasping the air. So damned thirsty.

JOEY KEEPS THE LIGHTS LOW to match the mood. Today, candles and a potluck finger-food brunch. It's meant to be a celebration but everyone in the room looks like they just buried a pet. To distract myself, I try to pick out who'll bolt for Pokanos; not an easy task. Everyone here's a candidate. Literally, everyone.

Joey's trying hard to make this party work though, I'll give him that. Seven layer dip, cheese plate, a bowl of fruit punch, virgin-style. The music: Van Morrison and Melissa Etheridge, the Eagles, some retro-techno band nobody knows. A silver tray of hotdogs sits on the table beside Phil, mustard in a glass bowl, homemade relish, a dish of fried onions. Nice touch, but I know Phil didn't bring them. He's eyeballing those dogs like they're gonna spark to life. Keeps checking his watch, fiddling with a cocktail shrimp, tapping his fingers on the frame of the Papasan chair he's gnarled himself into.

Joining the festivities today are the three rookies, each with less than six weeks under their belts. Marvin, Liza, and Raphael. Liza's husband brought her in the first time. She's tee-tering, an unlit Roman candle in a match factory. Raphael's an old guy, yellow-grey, cigarette-wrinkled, late to the party as it were. And Marvin, well, I know he's seen his share of ghosts. All three pigeons hunker off by themselves at the periphery, nervous and jumpy as hot oil. Someone's gonna run, I can smell it. The water wagon's tilted and covered in grease, a cinch to fall off. Even easier with a tiny, vindictive push, if things were to suddenly go awry.

STEP-PROGRAMS ARE A JOKE everyone's heard. Still, we base our recovery on these twelve pop-culture one-liners. Most of the steps, about as substantive as swallowing wind, but it gets real at number eight—make a list of the people you screwed over. The big trip down blackout lane. Currently, I'm pinballing between steps nine and twelve; making amends to the people on my list and spreading the message. It's not a linear thing, you bounce around a lot. Like sidewalk hopscotch, recovery leapfrog for addicts. One, two, three, jump! *Jump!*

Crystal would've appreciated the patience in a thing like this. She kept hoping things would get better between us, waiting for the real Lewis to emerge. Like watching a wriggly, grub-coloured cocoon and expecting butterflies to burst forth any second. One thing I loved about Crystal, the notes she left on the counter for me to find. One word at the start of each week, a different character trait she admired and thought I had. Diligence, devotion, bravery, faith. All nonsense, of course, a product of Crystal's nearly-endless optimism. Key word there, nearly.

I'm trying to write her a letter but how do you start something like that?

Hi Crystal, I know it's been a while, but I'm in this program, see? And I'm stuck on step nine...

Truthfully, I haven't seen Crystal since Kimberly's funeral. We never talked at the church, of course, or the cemetery. In fact, we haven't spoken a single word to each other since that day.

THEY TELL US GRIEF HAS A STEP PROGRAM of its own, each stage as intense as a roomful of parrots. And anger, Jesus, anger's the strongest of them all. This isn't the anger you feel when someone steals your parking spot at the mall. This anger compels you, gives you the authority to do anything in the world to ease the pain. The authority, even, to take someone's life should vengeance overcome you.

Here in Joey's basement, people carry their anger with them like a jam jar packed with fireflies. I've heard every one of their clenched-teeth routines. Hello, my name is Raphael and I'm an alcoholic. I set fire to my trailer, watched the aluminum siding hiss while I sang *Tim Finnegan's Wake*. Hello, my name is Liza. I sold my wedding ring for vodka martinis. My name is Phil and I put a dog in a microwave oven, (but only on defrost). Hello, I'm Lewis and I killed my daughter in a car accident, felt the muscles twitch even after her brain went out. But get this folks, here's the kicker—I was stone cold sober at the time.

KIMBERLY USED TO PUT A BLANKET over me when I'd pass out. She'd leave a glass of water on the coffee table and wait to see if we could go to the park. She loved that park—the swings, the dog run, the slide shaped like a corkscrew. That's the thing about kids, they don't hold grudges. They just squeeze everything they can out of each moment, cover it over with sweet, powdery sugar.

A week before Crystal left, I woke sprawled on the living room floor with one of Kimberly's blankets wrapped around me. I got up and searched for a drink, a pick-me-up, hair of the dying dog. Not a drop in the house.

Outside, Kimberly had set up a table and chair on the sidewalk. Handing out cups of lemonade, green Kool Aid, Fresca. A box of saltines on the table beside her. Smart kid, I thought. Get them eating dry crackers and they'll beg you for a cold drink. Only six, but sharp as cut glass.

It took me an hour to scrounge up enough money for a bottle and I was edgy when I left the house. Kimberly at her stand. Little wet circles on the tabletop. Sign taped to the front that read, *Lemonade Free*.

She poured a glass. "For you, Daddy," she offered. Look-what-I-can-do written all over her face.

"Free?" I said, looking at the sign. "Sweetie, what's all this?"

I still had the booze money curled up in my fist, tight as a spider's egg sac. "We can't just, you know, *give* stuff away. We don't have money to waste."

Kimberly just sat there.

"Do you know what waste is?" I said. My shirt half tucked, a yellow stain on my sleeve. I poured the lemonade she gave me on the ground in front of the table. "See? That's a waste." I dropped a stack of Premium Plus beside the spill, brought my runner down. Twisted my foot.

I could feel the shakes coming on. My mouth, dry as a vacuum bag. "Just charge something, okay?" I told her as I trotted off to the liquor store, cracker crumbs stuck to the sides of my shoe.

"HERE'S TO LEWIS!" JOEY SAYS. "A role model of perseverance."

There's a barren spit of applause from the room, a few soft-drink glasses in the air. Most of the group look away though and think about themselves. Understandable. For Marvin, especially. He turns his back and rubs his temples like he's trying to read the future. Jonesing bad and he deserves every gut-twisting rip. Right or wrong I wish upon him the all-powerful aches, the pain behind the eyes, the unquenchable guilt. Everything I experienced and more. Much, much more.

I bite into a canapé and reach for something to wash it down.

I don't think the newer members admire me, more like fear I'll look down on them now, a traveller in first class suddenly absolved of all my failures. The veterans know better of course; a milestone—doesn't matter what length—counts for less than a petrified turd.

I stopped drinking once before, on my own, not long after Crystal left. Not a sip for a whole month. I thought Crystal and I might get back together and I couldn't wait to tell her how good it felt. Food tasted better, even the air smelled different. Like surfacing after spending a year underground and someone hands you a bouquet of lilacs, some good tobacco, a bowl of cut oranges.

"I want to come back home," I told her when I picked Kimberly up. She stood in the doorway, hair tied back with an elastic.

My timing, so perfect.

Then Crystal said, "I'm sorry Lewis. Kimberly and I, we're moving to Richmond... but you can still see her. Weekends, in the summer too. I'm sorry. Please… I'm sorry."

WHEN I LEFT WITH KIMBERLY BESIDE ME, I know I wasn't right. Sober, yes, but not thinking straight. Would it have made a difference if I'd been clear-headed? Would anything have made a difference? It wouldn't have altered the path of the other driver. Or the position of the cocker spaniel we both swerved to miss. It wouldn't have changed the location of the light pole, the shattered glass that burrowed into Kimberly and me like ticks. If I'd been drinking that night—just a couple shots—would I have reacted differently?

I blamed the man in the Tercel, the one who knocked us off the road. Easier than blaming my own lack of attention or the dog that ran in front of us. Easier than blaming God—though my anger there was immense. This man became the centrepiece. The focus for my vengeance. Something I could touch.

Five months after the accident, I bought a couple bottles of Kressman white, alky screw-top wine. I went over to this man's house with the booze and some rocks I'd collected while scrounging for cans. The stones, palm-of-your-hand size, smooth as gunmetal. Ideal for smashing things. I hid in a row of junipers with the wine bottles on my lap, rocks in a pile beside me. All lit up like homemade fireworks with a lopsided grin and deep, flickering eyes. Anger makes you shine like that, makes you feel sober.

I sat under the bastard's window, rearranging the stones, numbering them with sweat from my forehead, cradling them like penguin eggs. I threw the first one to get his attention. It smashed through the middle of the glass and he came to the window, couldn't find me in the darkness. His face was backlit, confused. A perfect, guilty target.

I picked up stone number two and cocked my arm back. Slow and steady and spiteful as the hand of God himself.

SITTING HERE IN JOEY'S BASEMENT, I make the decision to leave out the twelve months of sobriety in my letter to Crystal. I don't want her to get the wrong idea and think I'm trying to reconnect.

Dear Crystal. There's no way to make amends for what I've done so I'm not even going to try.

Something like that.

Crystal *did* move to Richmond after the funeral like she'd planned. Inevitable, I know. Even if I'd been sober for a whole year instead of a month, she'd have done the same thing. If I could go back in time I wouldn't stop her from going. I wouldn't even try.

If I could change something though, I'd go back and tell Kimberly it's okay to give out free lemonade and crackers. I'd even help her set up the stand, organize the cashbox, pencil out the lettering. Then I'd sit back far enough so as not to interfere, and watch my daughter in action.

My daughter.

PHIL'S WIFE BAKED THE CAKE for the party. *Lewis* written in purple and blue, each letter struggling up a staircase of sticky white icing. Cute.

But my focus is elsewhere. Marvin, the newbie. Clutching his coffee with rickety hands, watching the door like a fox. I know he's thinking about the two-and-a-quarter miles to Pokanos, about sipping highballs under the benedictory grins of deer and moose. Although it's wrong, I'm glad he's hurting.

The accident: Marvin drove the other car. And I zeroed in on *his* face that night below the window with the rock.

I would have nailed him too if I'd thrown that second stone. But just before I launched it, he collapsed. Completely out of sight. At the time I thought maybe someone unscrewed the lid to the cosmic jar and knocked Marvin out of the way with His finger. I dropped the stones and ran. Sweating, tripping, drunk-stumbling. Not long after that I joined the idiots here, and—after 365 days of thinking mostly about myself— became an AA alumnus. A story so pathetic it makes me laugh. The story of the loser saved by God's greasy finger. The mason jar of forgiveness. The miracle of… what?

The tangible cause, of course, much simpler. Marvin was drunk that night, drunker than me. He passed out in front of the window in what can only be described as pisstank-perfect timing. I figured it out when I dragged myself to Marvin's place to apologize, to offer money for the shattered window. No one answered so I pushed on the unbolted door and found Marvin on the floor, naked and unconscious. Empty bottles beside him, legs folded like a toothpick umbrella. Wax paper spread out to catch the puke. Pretty inventive. I knew from experience, a bowl can be hard to hit.

Today is Marvin's fourth meeting. He surprised the hell out of me when he first showed up. A sucker punch, below the belt, gloves off. Even now, I can't believe he's here. Of all the gin joints in all the towns in all the world…

THERE HE GOES. Marvin, sliding along the wall of Joey's basement. Sweat beads all over him like the stink of bad judgement. I knew he'd be the one to crumble.

Joey brings in fresh coffee and Phil tunes the TV to a ball game. Then Liza starts weeping in the corner and everyone focuses on that. No one but me notices Marvin slipping away; I follow him outside.

Although the sun's beating down, there are ice chips under my skin. My whole body, numb. Marvin's at the bus stop in front of me, knocking his head against the shelter. When the bus shows up he almost breaks down the door to get in, exact change starting a fire in his hand. He sits in the back, right by the rear doors, and leans his head down between his knees. I creep in after him and scrunch into a seat at the front, across from the driver. I don't think Marvin notices. He's in his own world now.

The drive only takes minutes but the familiarity of the route makes it slow as hell. Soon as we reach Pokanos, Marvin jumps from his seat and slips out the rear. I get up too, from my hiding spot, and watch Marvin pause at the door, rub his hands through his hair, and then push through.

"Your stop?" the driver says to me, his eyes on the back of my head like a scalpel.

"My stop," I say.

DOMINGO'S SHAVED HIS GOATEE but otherwise nothing's changed. The bar still smells like a favourite chair; the air's still blue; the dead animals still pinned to the walls, stiff and sombre as a jury. Domingo nods to me and pours a shot of Jim Beam for Marvin. Funny, I never figured him a bourbon man, the bottles on the floor of his home were pretty random. I do know one thing though—Marvin was as sober as I was that night in his Tercel. The police tested us both.

That irony still makes me angry, mostly at God. A child picking up Mason jars, holding them to His pudgy face, giving them each a wild shake. Worlds falling apart over and over and over.

I walk to the counter beside Marvin, put my hand on his drink, pull it in front of me. The scent of alcohol quivers up from the glass, sliding around us, caressing our skin and telling us it's okay.

Marvin lifts his chin from his chest. "Oh Lewis. I'm, I'm…" He starts to cry, smacks his forehead hard enough to break a tumbler. He doesn't look like a killer. Doesn't look like part of a master plan either. And I start to think maybe it wasn't God who shook that jar after all. Maybe jars shake on their own, for no reason.

Marvin's right there on the edge with me. I lift the shot and do a mock *cheers*. Then I swirl the drink under my nose just like in the old days. My mouth opens automatically and I move the glass into position. The point of no return.

When the liquid touches my lips, I pause. Everything—the smoke, the stools, Marvin, the drink—suspends in mid-air like we're at the crest of a trampoline jump. I'm willing to wait for a second or two to see where the two of us might settle. In the sand, in the muck. Knocking into each other at the bottom of the trembling jar.

Marvin grabs my wrist. "Hey," he says. Then he says nothing and my arm remains frozen above the counter. This may be the start of a dialogue, maybe not. But today is *my* commemoration. And if there's one thing I have on my side right now, it's time.

THE CARTOGRAPHER

"**H**E'S ON THE LOOSE, Del, coming at you like a case of mange!" Jerry tells me. He shakes the newspaper and his double chin quivers as if full of baby mice. No surprise he's the first to sniff around; to Jerry, everything's a game of hide-and-seek.

"Is that right," I say, twisting the cash register key to *on*.

"More than right, my friend. It's a fact."

Jerry's a huge man, the kind they have to build special coffins for. He's got thin red hair, the landmine freckles of a Scot, and his accent, thick as fence paint, gets even worse on days like this when he has "a mission." He looks around for something to buy, settling on a box of construction-grade staples.

I don't tell Jerry, but I read the paper this morning too. Our rag's usually filled with articles about off-leash dogs at the park, the need for an increased snowplough budget, ads for the *Sub Shop* or my place, *The Good Little Hardware Store*. But today the front page held something different, and I knew it before I even got out of bed.

Jerry digs in his pocket for money while I put the staples in a paper bag. "Well, thanks for the sale," I tell him. He waits but I don't give him anything else. Finally, he turns to leave, stumbling on the mud-rug by the entrance. He catches himself, swings back around and blurts out, "If Satan was *my* brother, Del, I'd sleep with a shotgun for a pillow. I'll tell you that for nothing."

MARLER AND I ARE *NOT* BROTHERS. Identical twins, yes, but not *brothers* in any tangible sense. In fact, I haven't seen or heard from him since he left home at fifteen. Back then, Mom and Dad pleaded with me to figure out where he went.

"Where would you go," they asked, "if you ran away?"

"I wouldn't run away," I said.

"But if you did?"

"Why would I run away?"

Mom cried. Dad rubbed his hands over his eyes like he was trying to erase everything he'd ever seen. "I thought the two of you... I don't know. Don't you share the same thoughts or something? He's your brother for Christ's sake. Can't you at least try?"

I shook my head. "We're too different," I told them.

Three weeks later, they offered a bribe. "Fifty bucks," Dad said, waving the bills in front of me, "whether we find him or not."

"Wish I could help," I answered.

"What have you got to lose?"

"There's nothing to gain. It wouldn't be right to take your money."

A few weeks after that, they put an atlas in my hand. "Take a look," Mom said. "See what you make of it."

"I don't make a thing."

She handed me a pen. Opened the atlas to the British Columbia page. "Go ahead, Del. Follow the lines," she urged. "Start with our town, and then head to where you think Marler might be. Just let it flow."

"I don't think it works that way," I said.

"Why?"

"They're fixed lines. They end, cross over, go nowhere. And none of them say, *Hey look, here's Marler*."

"Extrapolate!" Dad said, loudly. "With a line of your own."

I flipped through the pages for appearance's sake, tapped the pen against my chin, then closed the book and handed it back. "Gave it my best shot," I told them. "Sorry."

It was a few more months before they finally gave up and accepted he was gone, that I couldn't *magic* him back. I guess I can't blame them for hounding me though, especially with the atlas. When we were young, Marler and I played this game with the *National Geographic* map in our room. We called ourselves cartographers as if we had control over the lines in front of us, the power to draw our own paths. One of us would approach the map and pick out a city or a lake, a bend in a river, anyplace at all. Then the other tried to guess. I chose places like the big island of Hawai'i while Marler went for the Kalahari Desert, the top of a huge, desolate mountain. And nine times out of ten, both of us, we'd nail each other's pick dead on. I know it seems impressive on the surface, the link Mom and Dad were hoping for. But it was nothing more than educated luck, a series of childish hunches. There's no way I could have actually tracked Marler down. No way on earth.

"HEY DEL," ROGER says, hitting his head on the brass bell hanging from the doorjamb. He's in full uniform today and I notice he's displaying his gun, unusual for him. He comes over to the counter, a small island that holds the cash register, a UNICEF tin, and a jar filled with liquorice for the customers' kids. I move the box of stock I was going through off to the side, fold my hands, and wait for him to speak.

Roger's been with the RCMP as long as I've been here, ten years now. In this town, his most strenuous duty involves pouring out open liquor at the Winter Fest. He has his business face on today though, square and impenetrable as a cinder block.

"Can I sell you a flashlight, Roger?" I say. "Cut a key for you?"

He takes his hat off and leans his elbow on the counter. "No."

He stands there, the space between us about the length of a tire iron. He's brought a copy of the paper with him too, same as Jerry, and he plunks it down in front of me. The photo of

Marler under the headline is an old one, a mug shot from when he first got arrested. There's a scab along one cheek and his eyes are dark as a slaughterhouse floor. Since this picture was taken he's been in and out of jail a bunch of times. Eventually, the papers started calling him *career thief, small-time lifer*. But after that last robbery, the one that went badly, *murderer* is what they call him now.

"Del," Roger says. "I'm sure he ain't coming. You know Jackson, he can't get the story right about which pair of jeans he put on this morning."

"Okay," I say.

In the article, Jackson wrote, *There's good indication escaped killer, Marler Wayne, will head to the Hardy Lake area where his twin brother owns and operates the local hardware store.*

He doesn't explain the *good indication* part.

"You realize Marler and I haven't seen each other in…"

"I know, Del. You've told me." He puts his hand up to block the rest of my sentence. "But still, let me know if you hear from him. The brother-connection thing can be pretty close sometimes."

"Not with us. Even the moons of Saturn are closer," I say.

Roger plucks one of the liquorice pieces from the jar and pops it in his mouth. He takes a long look at me, a stare someone might give a chess competitor. Then he nods and goes back out into the cold, jingling the bell again with his forehead as he leaves.

At five o'clock I flip the *closed* sign around, take the money from the till, and slide it into a brown envelope. There's a room in the back with a table and chairs, a microwave to heat up lunches, and a small, orderly washroom. I put the envelope in the cupboard strongbox, wipe the water-spots from the sink, and sweep the lunchroom floor. Then I find the newspaper on the table with Marler's face defying the whole world, and head back into the main part of the store.

There's a rack of maps set up beside the gardening section, mostly for fishermen passing through town to hit the river for steelhead. I grab one with the entire province and spread it out in front of me. The map resembles two hearts centred on the largest cities, the roads and rail lines pieced together like blood vessels, everything connected to everything else. I run my fingers over the entire thing in slow circles, giving special attention to the area around Hardy Lake, but I don't feel a thing. No quivers, no intuition. Just a slight tingling in my right hand, a bit of a cramp from a long day's work.

Someone knocks on the door.

"Hello?" I call out.

It takes a second to recognize the face through the frosty window: Jackson from the newspaper, squinting through the glass like he's examining a broken furnace. I fold the map, return it to the rack, and let him in.

"So, did you read the piece or what?" he asks. His glasses fog up immediately. "Front page and everything."

"What can I do for you, Jackson?" I say. "Sell you a hammer? Cut a key?"

"No, no. Just a few questions for a follow-up."

Jackson takes a fuse from the shelf and tosses it up and down in his hand, getting ready to give the big pitch he's been working on all day. I actually feel a little sorry for him. There's a gap between his front teeth that could house a Tic-Tac and a scar under his nose from a lousy cleft lip repair. Not to mention the obvious—Jackson really is a terrible journalist.

"I've checked into your past, Del. You're part of the neighbourhood Block Watch, you sponsor a foster child in Sri Lanka. And as far as I know you've never had a bad divorce or a long, drawn-out bankruptcy."

"Go on," I say.

"Okay, so tell me—how does it feel to have a killer right beside you, sitting on *your* pristine branch of the family tree?"

I sigh. "Marler and I are barely related. We're totally different people, we chose different paths, live different lives. We even had separate placentas, you know, in the womb."

Jackson nods his head. "I see," he says. "And when did Marler develop his taste for blood?"

"I don't think he... I don't know how to answer that."

He writes in his notebook, scratches his nose, and says, "You're not worried he'll come after you?"

"What?"

"You know, out of spite?"

"That doesn't even make sense."

"You're probably right," he says. "Why don't you tell me about your childhood?"

I LOCK UP AND WALK THE FEW BLOCKS to *The High Valley Food Mart*. The place is gloomy and it takes a second for my eyes to adjust from the twilight brightness of the snow outside. The rug at the door has slush stains on it, bits of gravel stuck in the weave, a chalky halo around the edge from the sidewalk salt. I wipe my feet and head to the produce aisle to begin my evening shopping.

When we were kids, Marler chose to sneak his vegetables onto my plate instead of eating them himself. That's one of the things I told Jackson. Along with having to do Marler's homework for him when he was failing Grade Six, returning the stuff he shoplifted, the pyromania phase, the gasoline-soaked tennis balls, the Grade Eight pregnancy scare that kept us both awake for nights scrutinizing the lines on the ceiling. I also talked about praying loudly in church so no one would hear Marler messing with the words. *Holy Mary, blessed art thou amongst women and blessed is the Fruit of Thy Loom, Jesus.*

I almost smiled at that last one, at how I looked out for Marler in small, weird ways. Then I came back to reality. Marler's a criminal. He and I aren't brothers, we're not neighbours. We're as separate and self-contained as two batteries and no matter how you slice it, nothing about his lifetime of delinquency is my fault.

My fault.

Dad actually said that once. He'd been drinking which, for him, usually meant Christmas or somebody's funeral. It had been six months with no contact from Marler and I'd just finished cleaning our room—*my room,* technically, because by then we all knew Marler wasn't coming back. Dad walked over and investigated the area Marler used to occupy; clean and tidy for the first time in years, the bed expertly made, comics and books stacked in the corner, the dresser dusted. To be honest, the order in the room felt pretty good.

Then Dad said, "Do you ever think that, being the way you are, it might drive people away?"

"Okay."

"*Okay?* You see what I mean? That's not even a normal answer. Not when this whole thing might be your fault."

He mumbled and left the room. And I tried to ignore what he just said, focussing instead on my newfound solitude, my comfortable privacy. My isolation.

In the next aisle, I run into Jerry examining a burlap bag of potatoes. He drops the sack to the floor and rushes over, much faster than you'd expect from such a huge man. Before I know it, I'm trapped in front of a row of boxed mandarins.

"Ah! Del," he says. "You're alive. That's good."

"Hi, Jerry."

He snoops in my basket. Puts his thick arm around my neck. "My friend," he says, "you should be buying bullets not broccoli."

"Thanks for the advice," I say, and I grind my teeth together hard enough to split a finger bone. Jerry doesn't notice; he just keeps talking.

"I don't know what gets into a crazy man's mind, Del. I can't read crazy-men-minds. But your brother's been stewing a long time. Thinking about all the things you did or didn't do. I've seen it before on TV," he says, pointing back and forth from one eye to the other. "Then there's the other issue, of course."

"What issue is that, Jerry? Can't wait to hear it."

"Well, you and Marler are *identical* twins."

I don't move, but my skin stiffens.

"Doesn't that mean you have the same genes? The same killer instinct, just waiting to come out?"

"Hey guys." Roger pops out of nowhere as if he's been watching us—watching *me*—the whole time. "How's it going?"

"Fine. Good. I'm good," Jerry says. He takes his arm from around my shoulders and backs away. "But not him. He doesn't even know the devil's coming and…"

"Why don't you go finish your shopping, Jerry?" Roger says. "And leave Del to his own." He puts a hand on Jerry's shoulder and I see the veins flex in his forearm, pushing up the hair on his skin.

Without another word, Jerry spins and walks off. He reaches down, jerks the bag of potatoes off the floor as easy as pulling a Kleenex from a box, and disappears around the corner.

I aim a little thank-you nod to Roger and force out a smile before continuing. If I had my way though, I'd grab a pineapple from the display, lift it in the air and smash it against the wall. Right beside Roger's big, fat, meddling head.

I WALK HOME IN THE COLD. My hair—damp with sweat from my neck—freezes into tiny ice-pick points. I pull my collar up and hope to God the street stays empty; I'm really not in the mood for any more encounters tonight. Another thing I think as I stomp along, I never should've done that interview with Jackson. He's only going to misinterpret things the way Jerry and Roger did. Except in Jackson's case, the whole town gets to read his pathetic drivel. I'll tell you this much, I don't feel sorry for him and his cleft-fucking-lip anymore.

Maybe the thing to do is craft a letter of my own. Send it off to the editor of the paper. "That'll put a stop to it," I whisper. "And then the final touch, when Marler gets arrested and put back in…"

I stop dead, two feet from the hardware store. Somehow I took a wrong turn and ended up here. A shiver goes down my back like a fuse. I rub my eyes, scrape the frost from the window, and unlock the door.

It's dark inside so I put the grocery bags on the ground and flip on a light. The cash register is untouched, the merchandise intact, everything seems normal. That is until I look down. On the floor in front of me there's a scattering of small dirty puddles. Footsteps of melted slush.

He's here, *right here*. Somewhere in the shop.

I follow the trail through the store into the back room. Empty, but there's a large puddle under one of the chairs. A carton of milk from the fridge sits open on the table and I notice the bathroom door is closed. I try the knob. Locked tight.

I lean my ear against the door, carefully, and spread my hands out on the wood. I can't hear or feel a thing. No quivers, no intuition. Nothing.

I concentrate harder and this time I do feel it: a slight tingling in my palm, like holding onto a jar of dragonflies. He's behind the door. Listening against the wood the same way I am. I feel his hands—calloused from scrambling through junkyards and pawn shops—moving over the surface. His breath, his heart, both racing in rhythm with mine, measured and perfect as a surveyor's level. There's the irrational urge to apologize but I don't know what for. I can't decide which feeling is strongest, which emotion to act upon.

Then I hear a noise.

The bell from the front entrance. And the heavy thump of footsteps in the main part of the store. I back away and head into the shop, closing the lunchroom door behind me.

Roger takes off his cap and stands by the counter, his gun picking up the glint of the overhead lights.

"Hi Del."

"Hi Roger. How's it going? Cold out there I'll bet," I say. "Can I sell you a wrench? Paintbrush? Putty knife? Cut a key for you?"

Roger turns his head to one side. "You okay, Del?"

"Yes," I say. "I'm okay."

"I noticed the light on in the store. Bit late for you, isn't it?"

"Yeah, well. No rest for the, ah…"

Roger nods and walks over to the peg-board in the corner, runs his fingers across the light switches, gang-plates, and dimmers. His hand moves down and brushes against his pistol.

He wanders towards the back room. "Mind if I take a look?" he asks, but he's not really asking. He keeps walking, and quietly unhooks his holster. Then he turns and goes through the doorway into the lunchroom.

I pick up a hammer and follow him.

"Bit messy in here," Roger says. "For you I mean."

I don't answer. The door to the bathroom is still closed.

Roger notices and takes his gun out of its holster, reaching for the doorknob. I tighten my grip on the hammer, sizing up the flesh between Roger's neckline and the collar of his coat.

"Locked," he says. He turns around to see me holding the mallet and wrinkles his forehead.

Everything is deathly quiet. I take a step forward so we're an arm's length apart. "Yeah," I say. I lift the hammer and use it to point at the door. "I was about to fix that. Been stuck for a while."

"Why don't I help you," he offers. "We can open it together."

He waits for me to make a move, but what can I do? No question Marler can hear us though the door. But there's nowhere he can go. Roger switches his gun to his left hand and takes a butter knife from the drawer beside him. He wedges it beneath the hinge-bolt and motions to me with the pistol. "Let's do it," he says.

I walk over, gripping the hammer tight enough to choke a kitten. I start tapping the handle of the knife. The bolt comes free and we do the same with the bottom one.

"Take the door off," Roger says.

When I hesitate, he lifts his gun. I put the hammer down, take hold of the door, and lift it off its hinges.

The bathroom is totally empty.

Roger and I take turns searching for evidence, silent and focused, like we're dragging the bottom of a lake. When we're done, I turn away to hide my blood-filled cheeks.

Before either one of us can speak, there's a crash from the front of the store. "I've seen him! I've seen him!" a voice calls.

We race around the corner and find Jerry doubled over, wheezing. He's upended the rack of maps and guidebooks and they're sprawled across the floor like mousetraps. Roger puts his gun away and goes over to him. "Jerry, what's going on?"

"I told you," Jerry insists. He waves his massive arm towards the east side of town. "Running like a ferret down by the McKesson place. Your devil-brother, Del, just like I predicted."

Roger stands silent, waiting for everything to sink in. Finally, he says to me, "You should probably stay here." The two of them go outside, jog down the street, and get into Roger's cruiser.

"WHY DID YOU COME?" I whisper.

There has to be a clue somewhere. A letter, a note, a one-word explanation. I check on the lunchroom floor, under the table, in the fridge. I even peek inside the stupid milk carton. Nothing.

The strongbox sits like a casket in the open cupboard and I bring it over to the table. The cash envelope is still there. And the money, inside.

I stuff the envelope in my pocket and head back into the deserted store.

Everything's normal except the floor, littered with maps. I get on my knees and sweep through them until I find the local one, the one of Hardy Lake. I clear a space and start unfolding right there on the floor. "C'mon, c'mon," I say. The map gets caught in a crease, tears a little, and finally opens. I flatten it out on the ground and start rubbing my hands up and down the streets, over and over. But I can't sense a thing.

I slow down, take a deep breath and look at the map again; it's indecipherable, as meaningless as a genetic code. Still, I reach out and gently touch it with both hands. It'll work, I know. If I just concentrate hard enough. Follow the lines that brought us here and extrapolate with a line of my own. Find that place where everything connects to everything else, where the flicker on the map *isn't* the Gobi desert or the Karjiang mountain, but the dirty motel room, the dumpster behind the post office, the lakeshore gazebo. That's where he'll be.

I wait for a sensation. But all I feel is slush water from the floor soaking up through the paper, dampening the street names. Smudges of black ink all over the tips of my fingers.

HOW TO RESCUE A BEAR CUB

1. GET THE FACTS.

Mom says, "There's a stray cub in the acreages. Tom Foster's dog chased the sow away and now the simpleton's been feeding the damn thing—bread soaked in apple juice. *Stay away from there. Understand?*" Dad shifts his pipe to the side and says, "Listen to your mother." And later when I tell him, my friend Jude says, "No way. A bear? What the hell are we waiting for?"

2. GATHER MATERIALS.

Jude lives with his father. His dad's a carpenter but he's been out of work a while, lost his job after Jude's mom—also a carpenter—took off. Their yard is filled with odd cuts of wood, chicken wire, old tools, bottles. We collect the supplies we'll need and go inside for lunch. Jude's dad is at the pub so Jude makes us mayonnaise sandwiches with Cheezies; he doesn't wipe the counter before or after. We discuss strategy while we eat. Jude calls the cub, *little fucker*, and refers to Tom Foster as *the retard*. My sandwich, I notice, tastes like sour milk.

3. BUILD A TRAP.

My role in the construction is *holder* and *go-fer* because Jude's better with tools. He sweats and sticks his tongue out while he pencils measurements. I ask him if his parents taught him how to build and he stops mid-cut and stares at me for a whole minute. Pretty soon though we've got a bear box: plywood sides and a small wire window in front. It's good. Really good, and I go to high-five Jude but he's busy flipping through the phonebook. Then he goes in the other room and makes a call. "Can you check again?" I hear him say. And a minute later, "Yeah, whatever."

4. ENLIST REINFORCEMENTS.

"Think about it," Jude says. "You'll be a hero." Tom Foster seems to like that idea. He lives in a double-wide inherited from his folks, has a worker who checks on him regularly, pays for things with his government cheque. He and his dog, Hovercraft, inspect the trap like it could be full of bees. We tell him his truck can transport the bear to the dump afterwards, where all the other bears are. "Where the mother is, probably," I add, and for some reason the back of my neck burns. Tom rubs his chin for a long time, his forehead wrinkled as a curtain. Finally, he agrees. "Okay then," he says. "If you guys say so."

5. SET UP.

We dump some bread in a bucket. Add apple juice, honey, and raspberry jam. We put the bucket in the box, and the box in the overgrown orchard. When it's done, Jude asks Tom if he can use the phone. "There is no phone," Tom says. He smiles and leans forward to let his dog lick his teeth. At first I'm worried Jude might crack him in the head while he's down there, bust a window or something. Instead, he sits on the sofa and mumbles to himself. I listen, but all I make out is: *should have left a note, fuck it anyway,* and *why should I care?*

6. EXECUTE THE PLAN.

We wait. Tom feeds us Pic-a-Pop and dry crackers while Hovercraft sucks up floor-crumbs. Then Tom brings out a deck of cards but Jude says, "What? Are we ninety?" so he sits there and whistles instead. After a while, Tom asks, "Do your Moms and Dads know where you are?" and the room goes silent, instantly filled with dirt. Before anyone can answer the question, Jude stands up and points out the window—a small, black shape wobbles towards the box. "Little fucker," Jude whispers. "And... also... *Holy shit.*" The dog starts to growl.

7. TAKE ACTION.

"Come on!" Jude steps out onto the porch, facing the orchard, the box, and the woods beyond. We follow him and stand side-by-side, Tom holding the dog back. The cub is small, harmless, like a stuffed toy parked next to the box. I want to say that to Jude but he's focused on the edge of the forest. Suddenly Hovercraft barks; the cub runs into the trap and the door shuts behind it. It works! It actually works! But instead of celebrating, Jude jumps off the porch, picks up a stick and yells, "Goddamn it." He starts running for the trap, full speed, and Tom and I finally see what he sees. The mother bear, on the far side of the orchard, emerging from the depths of the trees.

8. RECONSIDER.

The sow makes a huffing sound, deep and menacing, an earth-quake of a noise. She lumbers towards Jude; he doesn't back away. Instead, he goes over to the trap and tries to open it with the stick. The mother stands on her hind legs and bellows, starts moving faster, but the door to the trap is stuck. Jude hits the box with his hands, tears at the wood, pokes his fingers through the gaps in the wire. Tom can't take it anymore and closes his eyes. The mother bear lumbers forward, a couple more steps. And I don't know what to do.

9. Switch to Plan B.

We don't have a Plan B. The bear's nearly on top of Jude. "Should we sic the dog?" I yell to Tom, whose eyes are still closed, his face contorted. "Don't sic the dog," Jude calls out. "Just... don't." He leans his head down as he works on the box, the mother bear not ten feet away. I try to free Hovercraft anyway but Tom's too strong and the dog is thrashing back and forth, digging his claws into the painted wood of the porch. The bear stops in front of Jude and roars. The cub screams too, like a boy with a smashed thumb. Over the noise I hear Jude yell, "Not this time! Not this time!" and I nod like I understand. Then I punch Tom in the arm and yank the collar again; Hovercraft races towards the bear. When he gets there, the sow backs off. But then she takes a swipe and the dog tumbles, head over heels, making no sound as he rolls across the ground. No sound at all. "Hovercraft!" Tom cries. The bear turns back to the box, to its screaming cub. To Jude.

10. Keep faith.

My parents only take me to church for three things: Easter, Christmas, and the weddings of my older cousins. Still, for some reason, I fold my hands in front of me and look to the sky for intervention. Before I whisper a word though, a vehicle appears—my parents' truck, roaring up beside the porch. The sow steps back as the truck comes to a halt, shuffles close to Jude while the horn blares and plumes of road-dust creep across the orchard. Then she turns and runs off. "Wait!" Jude screams. "Come back, *please*." He still can't open the box. Tom runs over to his dog and picks him up. My parents get out, along with Jude's dad, and they rush over too. The cub stops yelling. Jude falls to his knees, buries his face in his shirt. And the mother bear disappears into the forest.

11. Evaluate the mission.

I don't see Jude for a few days. When I do, he's walking by the bus station, dragging a suitcase and eating a chocolate bar. "Hey," I say. But he just continues on. At first I want to rush home and tell my folks about him, make a phone call, tell *someone*. But in the end I stand there and do nothing. That night with the bear, my parents cried and hugged me, tears falling on the sawdust in my hair; Tom bandaged Hovercraft's injured leg; and Jude's dad smacked him in the back of the head. "You fuck-up," he said. "You know, you're the reason..." Then he and my father dismantled the box and freed the cub. It ran off in the direction the mother went, more or less, and we climbed into my parent's truck to go home. Tom Foster waved goodbye to us from the porch and I wondered what *his* parents were like when they were around. Angry? Mean? Or nice to him the way he's nice to everyone else? We pulled away while Tom sat quietly on his steps. Rocking back and forth and nuzzling his dog, singing to it as if it was a child. As if it was a present, something precious. All he had in the whole entire world.

PATIENT APPRECIATION NIGHT

I DON'T MISCALCULATE and I don't forget details. Instead, I catalogue events in my mind, preserving them like fine crystal. I'm not talking *idiot savant* or anything like that, I just like it when things are in order. And if they're not, my brain puts them that way for easy reference later on. Specifically, times like these.

That's the first thing I'll say at the hearing today. Then—because it could have happened to anyone—I'll tell them the whole story, beginning with the drive to work.

I was pacing myself so as not to arrive at 7:42 or 7:51. (Numbers that add up to thirteen.) I'm not superstitious but in my profession why take a chance? The man in the car behind me, however, didn't appreciate the rational caution, fingering me incessantly after we missed the green light at Cardinal and Oak. I waved and smiled, shrugged my shoulders politely. For all I knew he was my eight o'clock crown prep or new patient exam. This *is* a small town after all and business has to come first.

The timing of my arrival, perfect; exactly 7:45 on both my wristwatch and the dashboard clock as I pulled into my spot. I felt righteous, justifiably so, as I walked through the foyer and into the office.

"Good morning," I said to my receptionist, Sharon, sitting professionally at the desk with a stack of charts in front of her. She'd gone through them already and clipped a procedure checklist to each, highlighting any irregularities.

"Richard," she replied, nodding and returning to her work.

Sharon's not much for conversation but she's a marvel with patients. Listening earnestly while someone talks about their cracked tooth, but when it's time to pay the bill, unflinching. You can't train that kind of terrific. Sharon's my business touchstone and when I think about it now, I really should pay her more.

By the time I'd changed, everyone was waiting in the staff room for the first of our daily meetings.

Ranjeet, my hygienist, sipped a cup of tea in the chair beside me, six months pregnant but reliable as a work boot. When she first told me about the baby I immediately started calculating lost revenue for the practice, the hassles of hiring a temp, or worse, replacing her permanently if she decided not to return. But then her husband opted for parental leave and suddenly everyone was a winner.

Jennifer, my dental assistant, passed around a stack of photographs. I didn't have to look to know the theme: bridesmaid dresses, honeymoon locations, et cetera. That day, specifically, tiaras. I looked at the pictures out of consideration, of course, but nothing about weddings or relationships was on my radar. I think it's important I point that out.

"Time to focus," I said clunking the charts on the table like a gavel. "Let's see what's on deck, shall we?"

Sharon sat across from me and motioned to my tie which needed tightening. I know she does the same for her husband to whom she's been married twenty-seven years.

"Chair one, eight o'clock: new patient. Please note the latex allergy," I said, starting the meeting. "Chair two, eight-thirty: composite MOD, quadrant two. And I've given us an extra fifteen minutes for this one, Jen. You know Mrs. Evans. Expect to hold her hand the whole way."

I went through every patient like that, drawing attention to things like a colour mismatch on a $2400.00 crown and bridge (the lab's fault, not ours); a cell phone answerer who doesn't like the chair inclined; a four-year-old in for her first visit, the family infamous for *helicopter-parenting* each of her older siblings. Dentistry is stressful, yes, but stress can be mitigated by preparation, the reason for these meetings. We do a second one after lunch as well because nobody (except me) can remember the details of the whole day at once.

"Another thing," I announced at the end, "don't forget Thursday, *Patient Appreciation Night.* The caterer this year is Canterbury Cuisine and I'll provide wine from my home collection. Staff participation is expected. After all, you know the dictum, *if you're not building the business, you're building the roadblock.*"

"I'VE SEATED YOUR FIRST PATIENT," Jennifer told me. She hummed to the classical station we play in the office, an annoying but bearable habit. The clock beside us read 8:05.

"How are the wedding plans coming along?" I asked.

"Couldn't be better. You saw the tiara right? Also, my mom found a place that does personalized seashells. And I said, *Hello! Centrepieces!*"

"Sounds lovely, Jen. Really." And I thanked God when the clock changed and we could begin the day.

I read the chart on the way to the operatory. Jessie Lawrence. Thirty-one-year-old male. Chief complaint: discomfort, upper left. Not satisfied with previous dentist. Sounded easy. I put on my game face—sharp academic eyes, relaxed lips for calmative effect—and entered the room.

But I stopped when I saw the stockings, legs, and heels of Jessie Lawrence. The wrong box had been ticked under the gender heading. I don't like errors. Not even small ones. I handed the chart to Jennifer and pointed out the mistake for her to correct. Then I addressed the patient.

"Hello. I'm Dr. Richard Farrell. Glad to meet you."

"Hello Doctor," Jessie said, leaning forward to shake my hand.

I made a mental assessment while I masked and gloved up. Professionally dressed, a dental plan under her own name, long auburn hair with a controlled wildness. Trendy glasses, a lovely symmetry to her face, and an ideal smile.

I also admit noticing she was quite attractive. But anyone with eyes would notice that.

"How can I help you today?" I asked. I didn't dry my hands well enough after washing and the vinyl gloves stuck. I had to tug each finger separately like a rookie to get them on.

"This tooth hasn't been right since the last dentist did a filling." She touched her second bicuspid, number 2-5. "I've only seen him once, picked the name out of the phonebook when I moved to town. I have to say the first impression didn't bowl me over. I guess I'm looking for someone who's, well, perfect," she said, laughing. "Whatever that means, right?"

I knew the previous dentist she was talking about—perfect was the last word I'd use to describe that corner-cutter. A simple redo of the filling using a proper base would fix the problem. First things first though, I went through my standard new-patient routine. Step one: smile genuinely (people can tell if you're faking it even under the mask). Step two: casually glance at the wall with the framed degrees and multiple award certificates. Step three: provide a reassuring yet professional pat to the arm. And finally, use the patient's name in a comforting sentence.

"Don't worry Jessie, you're in the right place now. Let's have a look."

THAT EVENING I DINED at *The Royal*, a restaurant in one of the high-end hotels by the beach. I ordered halibut with cream sauce, roasted vegetables, and basmati rice. Then I slid my feet back and forth inside my Italian Derbies while I waited—I wear two pairs of socks in the evenings to help relieve the tension of a stressful workday and that night I chose one pair silk and one cashmere. Once in a while it's nice to treat yourself.

When the waiter—a fellow named Matthew with a dotty ant-trail moustache—brought out my meal, I noticed there were thirteen capers on the plate. I removed one of them before eating and left it in the empty place across from me. Otherwise everything was perfect.

When I was young, I never owned a bicycle, never played sports, never had a serious girlfriend. Instead I put all my energy into schoolwork, university, and then career. Working towards the day when nice cars and hotel restaurants became my norm. Now, at forty, with both my house and the dental practice paid off, I've made it. The good life. I don't even have to think about whether I'm happy or not. It's a no-brainer.

I considered the path of my life quite often over dinner. But that night my attention turned to Jessie Lawrence.

The gender error in the chart threw me off, yes. But there were other indelicacies on my part as well. I spent extra time on the head-and-neck exam even though her lymph nodes felt normal. I took more care than usual in the examination of her dentition making myself four minutes late for the next patient. And although Jessie's discomfort was mild, I had Sharon switch the next day's schedule so I could redo her restoration on an emergency pretense.

The reason for all this, I decided over a second glass of Russiz Superiore, was simple. I knew from experience things aren't always as they appear and I had a funny feeling about this case. Call it dental intuition if you like. It's the only reasonable explanation and looking back on the episode, I was right on the money about it, wasn't I?

The panel will have their own ideas of course. Yes, Jessie was attractive. And yes, I knew she was single, (from the personal information section of the chart). But being the quintessential professional, my office is neither a nightclub nor a coffee shop. Besides, I wasn't about to break my number-one rule no matter how lovely Jessie was: *never, ever, become romantically involved with a patient.* End of story.

THE NEXT DAY I INSTRUCTED Jennifer to give the operatory a double spray-down before Jessie's appointment. The previous patient left behind the maggoty smell of gum disease and I didn't want Jessie's first impression here sullied. I was being business savvy. And for the same reason I cleaned the specks from my glasses, washed my face, and rinsed with Listerine in the staff room before returning to the operatory.

Jessie sat in the dental chair reading a magazine. There were tons of *People*-type publications in the rack, yet she chose the latest edition of *The Economist*. I pay attention to these details to help guide conversation and devise appropriate treatment plans, essential in building a solid practice. It's also the reason I stood behind Jessie for two-and-a-half minutes in silence, watching her read.

She crossed her legs in an elegant manner and tucked a piece of hair behind her ear. As she read she ran her finger across the page, softly, like she was petting a ladybug. I smelled an apricot and vanilla fragrance from her shampoo. Strange, but I was sure it was the same kind I buy, a salon brand in a pyramid-shaped bottle. I had the urge to lean over, put my face right up to Jessie's hair. Just to see if it really was the same product or not. Out of curiosity.

Jennifer came into the room. I picked up Jessie's chart, cleared my throat and walked around to attend to the patient.

"Hello," I greeted her. "Nice to see you again. To get this problem dealt with."

"I'm glad you could squeeze me in."

I took a mask from the dispenser. My cheeks felt hot but I wasn't trying to hide my face, it's just more bona fide that way.

"Did the tooth bother you last night?" I asked, touching her arm in a professional and practiced manner.

"I can't lie, Doctor Farrell, it wasn't the best sleep I've ever had."

"Please, call me Richard."

I don't know why I said that, but I have to reveal the details exactly as they happened even if they embarrass me now.

For the anesthetic I used a piña colada flavoured topical, Articaine with a vasoconstrictor, and a 30-gauge needle, the thinnest I have. The patient tolerated the freezing well and I fully explained the procedure while it set in. Then we began. The old restoration came out easily and, as I suspected, there was leftover decay underneath that the previous hack had missed. Good thing Jessie was in my hands now, I thought. Good thing for her, I meant.

I kept the drill at the optimum speed while I cleaned out the cavity—too fast and the enamel scorches, too slow, like digging a grave with a spoon. Jessie closed her eyes while I worked; I pictured her, pain free, finally getting a good night's sleep. In my mind I watched her chest rise and fall as she drifted deeper and deeper. Her skin, smooth. Her breath, rhythmic. I wondered what it must be like to reach over at night and feel someone like Jessie beside you, warm, clean, pleasantly-scented. Something I've never had before, not even once in my entire life.

"Should I mix the base now?" Jennifer said, bringing me back to the moment. I'd been distracted, I admit. Lulled by the rhythm of perfecting the tooth preparation.

"Yes, I'm ready. Thank you, Jennifer." I gave the tooth one last kiss with the drill for posterity.

"How are you doing, Jessie?" I asked.

She nodded behind the silicon dental dam and—unable to speak—patted my knee to show me she was all right. It surprised me, the touch. But it was very reassuring. The achievement of a professional objective: rapport.

The rest of the appointment was textbook perfect. I put in a base, placed and cured the filling, and polished the surface until the new restoration was undetectable. And then, after checking the contacts of her bite, I did the same thing I do for all my patients—invited her to *Patient Appreciation Night*. My house, Thursday, 6:00 PM.

THE CATERED FOOD WAS QUITE ACCEPTABLE—salads, mini-quiches, chicken skewers and accoutrements—and I chose a variety of exceptional wines from my climate-controlled cellar to pair with the menu. I even had a few bottles of expensive port and ice wine at the ready, depending on who showed up and what their tastes might be. Always best to be prepared.

At precisely 7:00 I gave a short speech, showering accolades on the staff and thanking patients for their support. I mentioned a few plans I had for office upgrades in the coming year and ended with my usual line, "Everyone please enjoy yourselves. And remember, taxis *and* floss are both available at the end of the evening for whoever needs them."

After a receiving line of handshakes, I poured myself a glass of Château du Retout Haut-Médoc and retired to the side of the room to view the interactions between staff and patients, something a respectable host should do.

Someone spilled a drink on the hardwood and Sharon cleaned it up before I could even bring out a towel. Afterwards, her husband whispered something in her ear and she laughed, smacking his arm. Ranjeet's husband brought her a soda and rubbed her lower back while Rod Deacon, a long-time patient, pointed to her stomach and said, "If it's twins, you'll have to call them Rinse and Spit!" Jennifer, not to be outdone, showed off her fiancé as if he was a Waterford place setting, only letting go of his hand long enough to flaunt her engagement ring.

I should have been happy; my staff had many things going on in their lives. Instead, I felt disconnected. What did they say about me when patients asked? The only descriptors I could come up with had to do with work: studied, dexterous, exacting. Nothing else came to mind. Was the word *dentist* the sum total of my entire life?

At 8:00 I located myself by the front entrance so I could hear the doorbell if any stragglers arrived. I stayed there most of the night, interacting with patients as they walked to the washroom or toured the lower level. The doorway was quiet though, nobody else showed up.

And that nobody included Jessie.

THE ROAD WAS EMPTY on the drive to work the next day. I flipped on the radio for distraction but every song sounded like it came from a funeral home so I turned it off again and focused on the hum of the tires. I didn't feel melancholy or disappointment, just fatigue at having stayed up late to clean after the reception. The evening, however, had been a hit, that much I could claim. A record number of attendees, several promises for referrals, a few leftover bottles of wine back into the cellar for another night. Success. Still, I was out of sorts, which explains why I arrived at 7:51 and had to sit in the car for a while before going in.

"Richard," Sharon said from her usual perch, handing me the charts for the day.

"Hello Sharon. Did you enjoy yourself last night?" I asked.

"I did. Thank you."

She nodded. I nodded. But I didn't feel like saying anything else so I turned to go.

"Hang on," Sharon said. "Listen to this."

She pressed play on the answering machine and I perked up at the caller's voice. Jessie Lawrence.

"Sorry to be a bother, but there's a swelling above the tooth you guys worked on," she said. "I wonder if Richard could take a look. Please, call me."

"An abscess," I whispered. "Of course."

That's why she didn't come to the reception. I should have known there'd been a reason.

I re-examined her x-ray; no periapical evidence on the film so I didn't miss anything. Just one of those things, the tooth needed a root canal, that's all. Then I noticed Sharon had taken out the referral pad for Dr. Jacob, the endodontist we used in these cases. She held out a pen and when I didn't take it, she pushed it towards me and raised her eyebrow.

The truth is I didn't want to fire the patient off to someone else prematurely. I wanted to be thorough, cover all the bases, do what I was trained to do—help people with their dental needs.

"Reschedule my day," I told Sharon, "and give Ms. Lawrence a call."

I FOREWENT THE AFTERNOON STAFF MEETING so I could prepare for Jessie's root canal. I hadn't performed one in years and wanted everything to go smoothly. More to the point, I wanted everything to go *perfectly*. Jennifer tracked down the obturator and endo files from our storage room and sterilized the equipment while I studied the x-ray further. After everything was ready, I waited. Staring at the oracle-face of the clock on my desk; the slow, relentless tick of the second hand.

When Jesse arrived, the blood in my veins sparked. I put it down to nervousness at having to do a procedure I hadn't done in a while. Like riding a bike again, I suppose, after years of abstention. Those preliminary jitters when you first put your feet back into the pedals.

"Hello Jessie," I said in the operatory. She held her cheek with one hand, the universal sign of a toothache. She managed to smile anyway, a beautiful smile, despite her discomfort. I remember that detail clearly.

"I had an awful night," she whispered.

I almost replied, *Me too*. But stopped myself in time.

"Can you fix this, Richard?"

"Yes," I told her. "Definitely."

And there was nothing in the world I wanted more than to do just that. To make Jessie's pain go away. I wasn't even going to charge her for it. That's the honest truth.

I leaned the chair back and put my mask and gloves on. I touched Jessie's arm, gently, in a professional manner. Even though she hadn't slept, she still presented herself beautifully right down to her charcoal high-heel shoes. Most people in this situation would have shown up in sweatpants and the first t-shirt they could find. But not her. Not my Jessie.

I examined the area around the tooth, palpating the tissues with my finger, and saw plainly the tooth was abscessed. I explained what we needed to do, giving her all the options. When she agreed to the root canal, I administered anesthetic and rinsed the injection site. Everything by the book.

"You'll be fine, now," I said, reassuring her, noting she was somewhat pale, not unusual after receiving an injection.

I turned to the tray setup—all in order—and had an interesting thought. Perhaps when this was over, I could take Jessie out for a complimentary meal. Call it a *Personal Patient Appreciation Night*, seeing as how she'd missed out on the real one. A work-related event, of course, something I could write off. A gesture of goodwill to help her believe in dentistry again after what she'd been through. I wouldn't be breaking my rule. I'd simply be building the business.

Jennifer started humming to the classical station again, Ravel's *Bolero*. I gave her a look to let her know we should be solemn, our patient in distress. But she stopped humming even before I scolded her. Her eyes widened and she pointed at Jessie. "Something... Something's happening," she said.

I turned. Jessie's face was no longer pale, it was erythematic.

Splotchy as a failed kidney. Her lips and eyelids, swollen. Tiny welts around her mouth like bee stings. She tried to speak, but all that came out was a wheeze.

She was going into anaphylactic shock.

"Why?" she said, finally. Reaching up to her throat.

I asked myself the same question. I'd given the correct anesthetic, hadn't prescribed antibiotics yet, hadn't even started the root canal. Then I looked at Jessie's arm where I had just touched her a moment ago. There was a rash. A raised, red outline the exact size and shape of my hand.

Chair one, eight o'clock: new patient. Please note the latex allergy.

"What have I done?" I whispered.

A mistake, I admit. But forgivable? Given the circumstances, my pristine record, all my good intentions?

"Jennifer, get the EpiPen. *Now.*" I snapped my gloves off, threw them as deep into the trash bin as I could, covered them with paper towel. But by the time Jennifer returned with the adrenaline, Jessie's throat had already closed. She slumped back in the dental chair and slipped away from me, into unconsciousness.

It's TIME. I'LL TELL THE PANEL the entire story and accept the consequences. There'll be fines, retraining, a suspension from the registrar. My staff will have to take time off too, and I feel especially bad about that. But then life will go on, such as it is. There'll still be the perpetual constant of patients when it's over. And I'll still be a dentist. Apparently, the only thing I'll ever be.

I straighten my tie in the rear-view mirror and push back a tuft of hair. Then I collect my file folder, charts, and notebook and take the keys out of the ignition. I'm ready to explain myself to the College of Dental Surgeons.

As I reach for the door handle, I see a woman across the parking lot getting out of her vehicle to buy a ticket from the automated meter. *Jessie Lawrence!* But she's not supposed to be here. These proceedings are closed, even to her. It's a disciplinary hearing, not a court of law.

She places her parking slip on the dash and retrieves a black leather portfolio, leafing through the papers inside. Then she starts walking towards the College office, with purpose, on a mission. Right away I know what her mission is: she's here to stick up for me, to speak on my behalf. Jessie, my defender. It's the only logical explanation.

After all, I did save her life in the end. Took the correct steps, followed emergency protocols. I even held her hand (after thoroughly washing mine) in the ambulance while the paramedics worked on her. And now, she's here to return the favour—maybe *thank me*—even though I haven't spoken to her in months. Even though I'm not her dentist anymore.

Not her dentist anymore...

I throw the files on the passenger seat, fumble with the door handle. Then jump out of the car and run towards her. "Jessie," I call. "Wait. I need to ask you..."

She stops on the stairs at the entrance and turns. She's wearing a professional pinstripe skirt, a confident air, sunglasses, black pumps, perfect hair. She's beautiful. Always beautiful. I can't read the look on her face from here but that's okay. What could possibly go wrong now?

I walk up and stand beside her. Smile, genuinely. Touch her arm in that practiced manner. Before I speak though, I check my watch. The time is 11:11. *One plus one plus one plus one*. If that isn't a sign I don't know what is. Unless of course I read it as *eleven plus one plus one*. In which case I should wait a minute before interacting, just to be on the safe side. But a minute is a long time to wait. A very, very long time.

"Doctor," Jessie says, putting her hand on my shoulder and leaning forward, guiding me to regain my focus. "We'll see each other inside. Okay?"

"Of course. That's what I was going to ask... say," I tell her.

She continues into the building. After the door closes and I'm alone, I sit on the steps to interpret the signals. She called me *Doctor*.

Could it be—for the first time in my life—I'm wrong? Legitimately wrong? And if that's the case, if it's actually true, the obvious question remains. *Wrong about what?*

IN WHOSE ARMS YOU'RE GONNA BE

T HE NEIGHBOURHOOD CATS are in a throw-down, claws, teeth, everything. Usually no big deal but Ricky has to work in the morning and it was my idea to shack up here in the first place. The problem, Kent and Jillie's over-preened *Queen*, in season for days. Moaning and crop-dusting her scent along the street, holding back her affections. I wish one of those toms would just hurry up and take her already, make a pronouncement. Do what Mother Nature intended.

Something tips over in the alley, crashing on the pavement. "Christ," Ricky says, his voice husky from sleep and cigarettes. Hair buzzed short to beat the heat. Here in our bedroom he reminds me of a hundred different teddy bears.

"I'll take care of it," I tell him, fumbling for my housecoat.

Outside, the cats have separated. The small one, an orange tabby, sits balled up on the sidewalk like a little plastic pumpkin. There's a scar across his back and his left ear is all mangled, in need of attention. The cat in front of him, a scrappy bobtail, hunkers down when he sees me coming; greasy dark fur, hair-trigger pounce, a stare that feels like a sucker punch to the chin. He's the one I chase. "Go on. Bother someone else," I shout as he skulks off down the street.

By the time I turn around, the orange cat is gone too, an oily spit of blood on the ground where he was sitting. I put my hand over the area. Warm and wet and gravelly between my fingers.

Queen, the instigator of the whole thing, is nowhere in sight, of course. But there's a light across the street at her *palace of feline temptation*, Kent and Jillie's house. They're still up, and through the shears I see people dancing in their living room. I can't make out the details but Marcus Frick's Dakota, his precious baby, sits in the driveway. Ocean waves along the side, gaudy fog lamps, plastic bug screen that says *Delivering The Goods*. Marcus is Ricky's boss and he's supposed to be at work in the morning too, same early shift as Ricky.

I wipe my hand on the lawn and go back inside.

Ricky doesn't move as I slip in beside him but I know he's still awake, trying not to think about the morning. A man needs a decent sleep to do his job right. I watch him for a long time, lying there, breathing. Then I put my hand on his chest and count heartbeats because what else am I going to do? I'm certainly not falling asleep again tonight. Not with everything the way it is, not with a million questions. Not with that image of cat blood stuck there in my brain, clear as TV.

RICKY YAWNS AND POKES at his bacon and eggs. If nothing else, Momma taught me how to cook. "Hot food," she said, "and a hot bedroom'll keep your man happy." Her one and only pearl and she says it even now, ten years after Dad left.

I put some fresh toast on the edge of Ricky's plate. I want to rest my cheek on top of his head too, but instead, go off to pack his lunch.

Ricky's been driving forklift these past six months. More money than EI and we've actually been able to save a little. He's going to be a mechanic eventually, working on heavy equipment, tractor-trailers, buses. Already a whiz with engines, all he needs are some classes at one of those community colleges, the kind with the auto shop built right in. For now, he works for Marcus's contracting company, *Northern Recycling*, cutting up plastic tailings pipe at the mine. The pipe's huge, big enough to crawl through and long as that Great Chinese Wall. Ricky cuts ten-foot sections with a chainsaw, quarters them, and uses a forklift to stack the pieces on a flatbed. And Marcus, he just sits in the truck reading *Hustlers* till it's loaded, then drives off to God knows where. Half the time he smokes up while he waits, offering the joint to Ricky who tells him, "Chainsaw, Marcus. Remember?"

Marcus's truck is gone from across the street and I wonder if I should even mention it to Ricky. And what about Marcus's wife, Doreen? It wasn't *her* he was dancing with last night. That much is for sure.

I just don't trust that guy. One time the four of us went drinking at the *Pick In Time Pub* after work. Doreen wore ass-tight jeans and a silk top that draped off her boobs like a show curtain. The boys smoked Colts and pounded pitchers of draft, an ashtray full of matches between them. After a while, Marcus smacked Ricky on the arm, scratched a business card across his goatee and said, "I'll tell you something Ricky, the happiest people I know are all having affairs."

Someone had just given Doreen a baseball cap and she was oblivious, trying to fit her ponytail through the hole. Then Ricky leaned over to respond and some joker at the pool table hollered, "Dick around!" at that exact moment. The whole episode doesn't mean anything, people say stuff all the time. Still, from then on, my guard was up.

WELFARE CHEQUES MUST'VE COME late this week—there's a lineup at the bank and there's never a lineup in a two-poke town like this. Collette West is there, right in the middle with her daughter clinging to her like a burr. Her husband, Paul, has been gone a year now, no one knows where. Today Collette and her girl have smudges of dirt all over their clothes, unwashed hair, filthy runners. It looks like they've been camping but I know that isn't the case. I nod to them on my way to pick up the mail.

The post office is a dark, bunker-style building with cement walls and long rows of numbered boxes. The place is empty except for Doreen—the last person I want to run into—dressed in a spandex bodysuit for her aerobics class, talking to the clerk at the far end of the room. I sneak down to our mailbox but she sees me anyway and comes over, focused and persistent as a yellow jacket.

"Liz," she says.

"Hi Doreen." She brushes against me as I look in the open slot. Empty, except for a copy of *The Bare Bones*, our local newsletter.

"Nothing bad in that thing about me is there?" she asks.

"No," I say. Then realize it's a question you're not supposed to answer. Talking to Doreen always makes me nervous and it's even worse after what I saw last night. If she asks anything about Marcus, I don't know what I'll tell her.

"Here's a plan," she goes on. "Have dinner with us tonight. The boys don't have to work in the morning so, no excuses."

My instinct is to say *no way, no how, not a chance*. But like it or not Marcus *is* Ricky's boss. "Okay," I say. "I'll check with..."

"Great. Six-thirty. Don't forget to bring your hunk."

Doreen yawns at the door, covers her mouth with her mail. "Sorry. Didn't sleep last night," she says. She waves goodbye and starts speed walking towards the Rec Centre, her spandex suit shimmering in the sun like fool's gold.

Thank God the pharmacy, the real reason I came downtown, is in the exact opposite direction.

OFFICIALLY NOW, I'M SIX DAYS LATE. I've always been irregular so nothing to worry about really. Still, a little confirmation would be nice. There's a whole lot to read on the drugstore packaging but the gist of it is this: *unwrap the stick, hold it between your legs, let loose.* The hard part is the waiting—ten minutes, it says. It might as well say forever so I place it on the counter and make a call.

"Hello? Who's there?" she answers after four rings.

"It's me, Momma."

"What's wrong?" Her knitting needles click into the phone and in my mind I see her hair, almost fully grey now, tied back like a pretzel the way she does when she's concentrating.

"Nothing's wrong. I'm just calling, is all."

"Ricky leave you?"

"Jeez Momma, no."

"Relax girl. I'm just asking. Men do that, you know."

"I know," I say. "I know."

I was twelve when Dad took off. He'd been out of work more than a year, caught in the first of the mine's cutbacks. Momma always had a meal ready when he'd return from job hunting or drinking plastic-cup draft at the White Eagle Hall. And at nights, there'd be pawing and grunting going on behind the navy blue curtain that closed off their bedroom from the rest of the place. In the end, I guess that wasn't enough.

"You want some advice?" she says.

"Okay."

"Don't fuck it up. That's all I gotta say."

"All right Momma. I love you."

"Kiss on the head," she says, and makes a popping sound with her lips.

I start to answer, to make a kissing sound of my own, but she's already hung up. I used to think the hum of a dial tone was soothing if you held the phone away from your ear. Like a whale song or the rhythm of a lullaby. But now...

I put the phone down and take a breath; the test strip is bare. No line. No baby. Negative.

I toss it in the garbage beside me. My stomach's in knots and I feel like throwing up but I can't tell if that's from being happy or not happy. Just to be sure, I grab the stick again. *There is something*, a faint blue stripe in the result box, hardly visible. But what the hell does it mean? What kind of answer is that?

I read the instructions once more but they don't help. All they say is—in much fancier words—*maybe you is and maybe you isn't*.

"I'VE GOT SOMETHING TO TELL YOU," I say when Ricky gets home. He sits on the futon couch and plunks his lunchbox down by his feet. His hair's glossy with sweat; his shirt, splattered with melted plastic flung up from the chainsaw. I hand him a beer and an ashtray and sit across in one of those folding aluminium lawn chairs, the only other furniture we have.

"Yeah, I've got something too." He lights his smoke with a silver Zippo and snaps his wrist to close it. His dad's lighter, Ricky stole it the night he left home on his sixteenth birthday. He slides it into his pocket and leans back.

"You go first," I say.

"Marcus asked us to go for supper tonight. Insisted, actually. You know how he is."

I get a sudden image of Collette West and her daughter standing all grubby at the bank. "That's what I was going to tell you, too," I say. "I ran into Doreen at the post office earlier. What a coincidence, hey?"

I try to smile but it's hard to keep anything from Ricky. He once told me he can smell the sweetness in someone's sweat when they lie, "like raspberry vinegar." But me, I can't read anyone, not even the person I'm supposed to be closest to.

"We better get cleaned up then," he says, taking a swig of beer. "Don't want to stink in front of the boss man's wife."

WE TAKE TURNS GETTING READY and although I don't *avoid* Ricky, I do avoid looking into his eyes. He's wearing the denim shirt I got him last Christmas that shows off his chest and arms; I settle on the same jeans from earlier and a light blue sweater. I put on some makeup for the evening too, first time in a long time. Eyes, lips, everything.

"Coming?" Ricky calls from the hallway. He's been quiet since his shower and it makes me wonder what Marcus said to him at work. What he says to him in general, for that matter. Like I said, I don't trust that guy.

"Hmm." Ricky looks me over when I come out of the bedroom. He taps his hand on his leg, downs the rest of his beer, and pulls open the door.

The cats from last night are lurking on the step. The mean one jumps back and hisses, crouching into ambush-mode. He runs down the street while the orange one goes off the other way. Queen is there this time too, sitting on the wooden fence between houses. I feel her darty green eyes zeroing in on us as we walk past her. Right up until we get into the car, roll down the windows, and drive off down the road.

"RIGHT ON," MARCUS SAYS at the entrance. He's greased his goatee to a fine point and left the top two buttons of his shirt undone. He gestures for Ricky and me to enter but we hesitate. Already, it feels like there's something in the air that could make a canary topple over.

"Don't just stand there," Marcus says. "Let's rev this thing up."

He guides us through the house to the living room, sunk down a couple steps into a carpeted lair. Doreen's blowing on an incense stick, wearing a black mini-dress as tight as the spandex she had on earlier. When she sees us, she twists her hips, spilling some of her drink.

"First drip of the night!" Marcus calls out. He sits on the couch in front of a bottle of tequila and pours four shots right up to the top.

"No thanks," I say. It comes out too quickly though, like a ginger ale burp. Stupid me, I didn't even think about drinking. I don't know what the rules are these days anyway. Or, in my situation, how those rules apply. Ricky twists his glass between his fingers. Then he downs it and shivers. Tequila's not his thing.

Before I can think of a good teetotaller excuse for the evening, Doreen dances over and sits between Marcus and Ricky. "No shoptalk tonight, you two," she says. "Orders."

"If we disobey?" Marcus asks.

"Well, if you guys are naughty, I will be too."

The room is spinning and the stink of incense, cigarettes, and tequila turns my stomach even more than Doreen. I have to keep it together though, for Ricky's sake.

"Doreen," I say.

"What is it Liz?" Her voice, fake as plastic sugar cubes.

"Where's your washroom?"

Marcus jumps up. "I'll show you," he says. Doreen stays right next to Ricky, their legs pressed together despite all the room.

"C'mon, gorgeous." Marcus puts his hand above my ass to guide me along. "To the powder room."

Their bathroom—a bright, glittery olive colour—smells like a mix of cheap perfume and deodorant soap. Dozens of candles sit on the counter and right above the toilet, a framed picture of fat Elvis sweating into a microphone. None of this helps my stomach much. I lock the door and place a cold washcloth on the back of my neck. "Just get through it, Liz," I whisper to my reflection. "That's all you can do."

By the time I get back, Marcus has brought out the pot. He wiggles a joint in my direction but I wave it off, casually. Ricky's had some already, I can tell. His eyes look like he spent the afternoon in a hot tub. It's been a while since he and I have been stoned together and I'll actually miss it if we have to stop. Pot itself doesn't do much for me but it makes Ricky extra affectionate, which I adore. Under normal circumstances, that is.

Doreen puts her arms along the rear of the couch behind Ricky and Marcus. She pats them both on the back. "Smoke up boys. Dinner's almost ready."

PAPER NAMETAGS ON THE PLATES tell us where to sit. "Boy, girl, boy, girl," Doreen sings, bringing out a tray of lasagne. Marcus floats in behind her and pours wine for everyone, me included.

"Cheers," Doreen says.

I take the tiniest sip I can possibly take, and we eat. When Doreen leans forward to reach for the salad, her ultra-tight dress almost disappears. Ricky glances at her but I guess I can't blame him. With everything out on display like that, even my eyes wander.

"Not bad, huh?" Marcus says.

At first I think he's talking about the food but he points his thumb at Doreen's chest. I nearly choke on my garlic bread.

"Ah, sorry?" Ricky says.

"Oh, it's okay. Feel free to look." Marcus rubs his hand down Doreen's back like he's stroking a leopard. "Flirting's okay as long as you remember who you're going home with at the end of the night. You know, like that song, *Save the Last Dance for Me*."

"Oh stop it." Doreen looks away but she has a sneaky smile on her face and she's pushing her boobs out farther. "He's harmless."

Ricky's head turns so I can't see the expression on his face. More importantly, I can't see his eyes.

"Should've seen us last night at Kent and Jillie's, right by your place," Marcus continues. He winks at Doreen and both of them go back to eating like nothing just happened at all.

No MORE COMMENTS ABOUT DOREEN'S BODY during the rest of dinner, thank God, but I think she tried some footsies thing with Ricky while she ate. Right now, she's fixing dessert in the kitchen with the boys jostling around her like seagulls. I don't want to leave them alone but I don't want to bleed all over either and my entire midsection feels hot and swollen. I excuse myself and head back to the washroom.

"Fuck," I say, seated beneath the disturbing Elvis picture. Still nothing.

I wish I'd read the instructions better on the pregnancy test. Like how long until you can try again, or how accurate the stick really is. I think about Momma and the stupid things she said on the phone earlier. Things I'd never say to a daughter under similar circumstances. Under any circumstances, really. But I can't waste time on unrelated concerns. I have to get back before our hosts pull something else from their big bag of uncomfortable party tricks.

I open the door. Marcus is right there.

"Hey Liz," he says, toying with his chest. After dinner, Ricky and him did a couple more shots and right now his eyes look like dirty little fishbowls.

"Where's Ricky?" I ask.

"That's a good man you've got there. I'm thinking about training him on some equipment. Maybe an apprenticeship. What do you think?"

It's a lie, that's what I think. But if he *is* telling the truth, what does that mean for Ricky and me?

There's a crash from the other room followed by Doreen's big fake laugh. Marcus takes a step towards me, his eyes crawling over my body.

"We better check," I say. "See what's going on."

Marcus doesn't move for a second or two, then nods and steps aside.

We find Ricky and Doreen on their knees in the kitchen, cleaning up a spill. From this angle, an all-inclusive look at Doreen's cleavage. "Drip number two," Marcus calls out.

"Hey, how about a pre-dessert smoke?" Doreen says when she sees us. "We're not all out, are we?"

"Sorry, Babe," Marcus answers.

I thank God for small favours. A little cake and we'll excuse ourselves, go home, climb into bed. Forget about everything. Then Marcus continues, "Well, there *is* my work stash, but I need a designated driver to get there. How about it, Liz?"

Ricky stops wiping but doesn't raise his head. I wonder if he knows about the apprenticeship idea or not. Either way, he isn't trying to stop what's happening now. He isn't sticking up for me. He isn't anything.

"All right," I blurt out. "I'll drive. If that's what everyone wants."

Ricky still doesn't budge. Not even when I walk past him to the door, with Marcus holding my arm. He just sits on the floor with Doreen, both of them silent, both of them fidgeting. A tiny space of air, the only buffer between them.

LIGHT POLES LINE THE ROAD to the mine, illuminating black circles of asphalt below. They're fewer and fewer as we get closer to the worksite, the old pit they closed off last year. Marcus hasn't said much during the drive but he's been singing to the radio, a classic rock station featuring an all-night AC/DC special. When *Have a Drink on Me* ends, he takes a long drag from his cigarette, lighting up the truck cabin; I don't have to look to know his eyes are scanning my body again in the pale orange glow.

We pull up in front of a small trailer with a plastic sign on the door that says, *Northern Recycling*. Marcus reaches over, turns off the engine and puts the keys in his pocket. "Headquarters," he says. "C'mon."

There's an old flatbed stacked with pieces of pipe beside the trailer. Next to that, Ricky's forklift, a garbage bin filled with scrap metal, and off to the left a long piece of uncut tailings pipe curving out between the trees. We go past everything, up the steps and into the building.

"The heart of *Northern Recycling*," Marcus says. He spreads his arms and gestures around the place. "Not much to look at, huh?"

I shake my head. There's a desk in the middle of the room where I picture Ricky eating the lunches I pack him. Then I notice a stack of dirty magazines and hope he eats outside. A tall bookshelf stands against the wall filled with plastic tubing and tools, a pile of twisted chainsaw blades. There's another desk in the corner, some chairs, a mud-caked runner rug, the smell of old mushrooms. Everything about this place is unsettling but what I'm really thinking about is what's going on at the house with Ricky and Doreen. Leaving him there feels like leaving a child in a store that sells only mousetraps.

"Better get the stuff," I say. "Everyone'll be wondering..."

"They're fine. Doreen's a born entertainer." Marcus pushes a chair over to the bookshelf and looks up at a small piece of plumber's pipe on the top ledge. "Give me a hand here Liz, I'm a bit tipsy. The pot's inside that pipe."

It's hot in the trailer and I'm feeling a little dizzy myself. But the faster we do this, the faster we'll get back to the house. So I climb up on the chair and hold the edge of the bookshelf for balance.

"Don't worry," Marcus says. He grabs my legs with both hands. "I got you."

I find a plastic bag inside the tube but it's stuck. "I can't get it," I say.

Marcus's hands slide up my thighs. "C'mon baby."

I tug harder. But nothing gives.

"You can do it," he says. His fingers start to pinch, squeezing the flesh through my jeans. I can feel the heat of his breath on my ass. Then I feel his lips, his goatee...

In one quick motion, I grab the entire chunk of pipe and jump down, twisting my ankle as I land on the trailer floor. The pipe spins off under the desk.

"Jeez Liz. You all right?"

My ankle throbs and my hip feels bruised. Also, I want

to cry but that's stupid. "I'm fine." I grab the chair and hoist myself up.

"Just let me get this stuff and we'll go." Marcus crawls under the desk and fishes for the pot.

While he's down there, I limp for the door.

I'm halfway down the stairs, heading for the truck when it hits me—Marcus has the keys. There's nowhere to go and it's way too far to run back to town. Instead, I hobble over to the big tailings pipe, kneel down, and crawl inside. The floor's covered in dust, cold as freezer meat. And the pipe goes on in total darkness, much farther than I can even imagine.

Marcus stumbles out of the trailer. "Liz," he yells. "Come on, Lizzy-Liz!"

I don't move or say anything. Frogs chirp somewhere near but the sound of Marcus's boots drowns them out, crunching on the gravel, getting closer and closer, deliberately slow and heavy. Eventually the footsteps stop at the opening and I hear Marcus tap on the outer ridge of plastic with his fingers. He starts whistling like he's calling a lost dog. But then I hear something else. The creaky sound of an old car door.

"Hey buddy!" Marcus says. "Didn't see you there. What's going on?"

My hands shake as I crawl over to take a look. *Ricky!* Walking towards Marcus, his car parked behind the trailer. I can't believe he was crazy enough to drive after us. He looks drunk as a parrot, swaying in the dim light. Tequila's really not his thing.

"There a problem?" Marcus asks.

Ricky wavers, but doesn't back away. "I don't like this," he answers.

"Did Doreen try some weird shit on you? Because…"

"I said I don't like it."

Marcus shakes his head. "I knew you'd be like this. I fuckin' knew it," he says. Then he shoves Ricky's shoulder, hard. He starts to say something else but Ricky launches a haymaker. He misses and nearly falls. In all the time we've been together, I've never seen him like this. He's vibrating, physically vibrating, with jealousy. The good kind of jealousy.

"What the fuck, man." Marcus ducks as Ricky takes another swing. This time he does fall. And Marcus hits him on the back of the head with the pot-tube as he goes down.

"Ricky!" I scream, crawling out of the tailings pipe and hobbling over.

Marcus drops the tube and backs away. "He came at me," he says. "You saw it."

Ricky's hair is soft and warm. There's a scuff across his cheek but otherwise he's unscathed. "Are you okay?" he asks, like I'm the one who's been scrapping. He wrinkles his forehead and says again, "You all right?"

For some reason I think about the used test stick in the bathroom at home, sitting in the trashcan between the toilet and shower. "Yeah Ricky," I say. "I'm good."

He gets up, goes over to Marcus and squares off again.

"Jesus Christ," Marcus says. "You work for *me*, remember?"

Ricky just stands there, strong and brave as a grizzly bear. *My* grizzly bear. I give them some room and very carefully climb on top of the tailings pipe. My stomach's much better in the fresh air and even though I should be scared, I'm not. In fact, this is the best I've felt all week.

"C'mon then," Marcus says. "Let's do it." He thumps his chest and does a one-two punch in the air. Then the two of them circle each other, moving back and forth. Sizing things up as they shuffle in and out of the darkness.

THE MIMIC

WHEN I BOTHERED TO THINK about it, which wasn't often, I imagined my father's home as flawless and pristine. A postcard house with geometric hedges around the perimeter, a perfectly cut lawn, windows reflecting the sun in bright, musical, hallelujah rays. No tire swings in the yard, no dandelions sullying up the place, no bikes, doghouses, not a hint of peeling paint. That, I admit, was my expectation.

But the house I'm looking at now…

I pull off to the side, listening to the tick of the car's engine. There's a broken fence spanning one edge of the property and an overgrown spruce along the other, its lower branches hacked away to create a small, passable tunnel to the backyard. In front lies a flower bed filled with knapweeds, thistles, piles of firewood neglected so long they've gone to rot. And the building itself: a brown bungalow with brown trim, brown stairs, and brown curtains in every tightly-shut window. The appearance of a flophouse or an abandoned hideout, a guilty place. But I didn't come here to judge.

"Helloo-oo! You must be Dierk's daughter. Wait there. I'll come over," someone says. It's the neighbour, Rita. I recognize her voice from the phone, the pitch high and sharp like the ping of a barcode scanner. She's a large woman, wearing a shapeless cotton muumuu dress with Eiffel Towers and French poodles all over it. When she gets close I smell the baby powder she uses to keep her flesh from rubbing together.

"Hello," I say. "I'm Elena Werden."

"Pleased to meet you." At first Rita offers a big smile along with her hand but then she remembers why I'm here and lowers her eyes. "Sorry for your loss," she says. "I've got the keys right here."

She hands them to me and stands there, breathing. Waiting for me to ask about my father's last days. Perhaps decide on the future of the house or explain why I've never visited though my father's lived here for decades.

"Thank you," I say. "This should only take a few days. I'll be in touch if legal arrangements require." I put the keys in my pocket and turn to get the supplies from the car. I move slowly, giving Rita plenty of time to leave. She stays motionless though, studying me like the eyes of a painting.

"Something else?" I ask, turning to face her.

"Oh. Yes, well, there's the matter of the bird, of course."

I wait for more.

"Your father's parrot. Must have slipped your mind with everything that's been going on, you poor thing. Don't worry. I'll wait until you're settled before bringing him over."

"Fine," I tell her. "That'll be just fine."

FIFTEEN MINUTES AFTER the conversation at the car, Rita brings over the parrot I knew nothing about. How could I know? I haven't spoken to my father since the day he left, back when I was nine years old. My mother hardly mentioned him and on those limited occasions when I inquired, she told me, "His choice, Elena, not mine. Just block it out. You'll get used to it soon enough."

That was her mantra right up until the day she passed, five years ago from an aneurysm of the heart. She shouldn't have worried about my *blocking things out* though. There was nothing to block—the only correspondence I received from my father came last month, his official death certificate and will.

Not that it upset me, being fatherless as a child; I was never the type to be thrown in the air or have my hand held while waiting for the school bus. My father's leaving only helped nurture that independence, turning me into who I am today. Really, if anything, I should have thanked him.

I help Rita carry the blanket-covered birdcage to a corner of the living room with Plexiglas on the walls, presumably for mess control. We manoeuvre the stand into the flattened circle on the rug and step back. A threadbare armchair sits to the left of the cage; behind it, a stack of newspapers. There's a remote lying on an ottoman, a TV on a silver base, and a tin-metal dinner tray at the ready. That's it. A dingy place with poor lighting and heavy air, the smell of an oily basement.

"Here's the food," Rita says, putting a bag of seeds on the floor and rubbing some dust off her hands. She looks worried, like she's selling me an appliance that doesn't work. "He's an African Grey and his name is Lowen. That's all I know. If you need anything else, just call me. I'm always around, dear."

"Thank you." I guide her towards the door before she starts hinting at afternoon tea or some other cordial absurdity. As soon as she's gone, I unpack my supplies. Paper shredder, the local phone book, laptop, a guide called *Duties of an Executor and Trustee*. Then I tape three garbage bags to the table and label them *goodwill, trash,* and *recycling*. It might seem obsessive but the more organized I am, the faster this will go. No feelings here to slow me down. No relishing of fond memories. I'd have the same level of connection scorekeeping a game of darts between two drunken strangers. And that's fine by me.

A scratching sound comes from the cage. The parrot, stirring.

I pull the cover off and Lowen, behind the bars, backs away. He's shabby and unkempt. A big grey mess. There are long patches of missing feathers on his body and if he wasn't the only animal in the room, I'd think he was being picked on. I lean towards the bird—the complication I'm forced to deal with here—and he turns his head to the side and squints at me like a border guard.

"What am I going to do with you?" I say, flicking my nail against the cage.

He opens his beak wide enough to take down a nectarine. "Awwwk. What are we going to do, Lowen? What are we going to do now?" he says.

My skin goes cold, the chill piercing the centre of my bones. Even though it's been a long time, there's no mistaking it: the voice coming from the cage—tone, accent, everything—an exact carbon copy of my father's.

JUST BEFORE BEDTIME, I put on some gloves to feed the ridiculous bird. He doesn't say anything else, thank God, not even a squawk. When I approach the cage with a cup of seeds and some fresh water, Lowen drops his head and we ignore each other during the entire interaction. Precisely the way it should be.

After picking at his food as though sorting through floor-sweepings, the bird settles down for the night. I do the same, rolling my sleeping bag out on my father's couch. As soon as I lie down though, I see water stains on the ceiling and splatters on the light fixture from a lousy paint job. It makes me want to scream so I close my eyes to block out the whole sickly mess. I think about happier things: the communications contract I just landed, sushi takeout from the new place on Cobalt, my minimalist furnishings. Eventually, I feel the tension in my jaw begin to relax. My neck muscles, loosening.

I actually start to drift off. Images of a dream take over and I'm too tired to fight them. I let myself glide, carried like a child from the backseat of a car. Floating safely through doors, upstairs, into a fresh warm bed. It's pleasant, almost musical. And it feels a little bit like forgetting. I lose all track of time in the dream and I'm not exactly sure what year it's supposed to be. Then I hear a voice. A whispering. The soft noise of someone crying.

"Elena," the voice calls me. "Elena."

I sit up, wide awake. The sound isn't coming from the dream, it's my father's voice right here in the room. I'm not stupid. I know it's only the bird. But still.

I hold my breath and stay motionless; all I hear is the rustle of the sheets, the water pipes, the crickets outside. Somehow this place has a way of making silence more powerful than it ought to be.

A few minutes later Lowen starts up again, filling the room with that voice. I let it wash over me and my skin tingles. The words get louder, the focus more precise. And my cheeks fill with blood when I realize it's not Elena he's saying after all. It's *Eva*, a name I've never heard associated with my father before. Not in the will, certainly not from Mother, not anywhere.

It continues long into the night, so softly it's almost inaudible.

"Eva, Eva, Eva."

BY TEN THE NEXT MORNING I've filled three bags with garbage, two with donations, and one recycling. I find some official documents in a drawer and put them in a pile for later. Everything else I shred with the efficiency and single-mindedness of an ant colony. I don't stop to read anything, don't ponder the items my father collected over the years—ball caps, ceramic fruit, sixteen different cribbage boards—and although I'm slightly curious about it, Lowen's weirdness last night changes nothing.

After a sufficient amount of progress, I sit at the table in front of the laptop to eat my lunch. While I'm at it, I make a list of some of the larger items in the house—the uncomfortable couch, the TV, the table and chairs—and enter their descriptions into Craigslist. Then I scroll down and click on the pets section. *African Grey. Complete with own cage and food. Make an offer.*

Lowen comes to life, running his beak back and forth against the bars like a tin cup. A coincidence, but I feel a tiny speck of guilt just the same. There's nothing personal in any of this, though, divesting an estate means just that. Nothing more, nothing less.

Lowen turns his back to me. I hit *enter* and move on.

Thankfully, I have an appointment set up with a realtor this afternoon; going through my father's debris is like trying to swim in a pool of dry-cleaner bags. I gather the will, the property title and the encumbrance certificate and put them in a folder titled, *Residence.* I don't see anything else essential to the listing, but I do find something curious hidden between the pages of a bank statement. An old life insurance certificate.

It's one of those no-medical-exam-TV-infomercial things with a pittance for a payout. The name of the beneficiary, however, has been scribbled over in ink. Crossed off so vigorously the paper's actually torn from the force of the pen. I smooth it out and hold it up to the light. Only the first name is legible and although there's no reason to feel this way, I get a little jolt when I notice it's not me. The name, instead, is the one Lowen whispered over and over last night in the dark. The enigmatic and increasingly annoying *Eva*.

I HAVE FOUR DISTINCT MEMORIES of my father. The first, my sixth birthday. My mother took pictures while Father held the cake. "You missed a candle, darling," he told me, though I hadn't really. "See here, Elena? Look close. A little closer." What's memorable is it was the first time I realized my father had an accent. I'd been so used to hearing his German frankness, the crisp pop of syllables, that it hadn't occurred to me before. The candle smoke wisped between us, disguising my father's mischievous grin. And although I knew exactly what he was up to I couldn't stop staring at his mouth, waiting for the next word to come out. I stayed like that, fixated on his lips, until he pushed the cake right into my nose. Rubbed icing all over my expectant face.

The second memory, Darden Lake. Walking out on *Grandmother's Arms*, the fallen, floating tree that had been there forever. There were branches coated in gelatinous moss stretching underwater in every direction. The wood was slick, the lake, clear and deep. "Go ahead. I'm watching," Father said, already at the far end of the tree, his hands reaching out to urge me on. I knew I was going to fall even before I took my first step. What I didn't know is whether I'd hit my head, end up trapped under a branch, sink like a stone. And when I looked to my father for reassurance, I couldn't tell if he'd dive in after me or not. If he'd actually be there to save me.

The third, my father sitting on the porch watching a thunderstorm at night. It was a month before the divorce, and he'd been sitting there a lot. I went outside to join him and the sudden clack of the screen door startled us both. "Come, Elena," he said. "Sit with me a while." The rain pounded on the corrugated roof, ran off the grooves in steady streams. I climbed on the bench next to him, smelled chewing tobacco on his breath, spiced apples and new leather. Despite the coolness in the air, his body heat kept me from shivering. I remember a lot of lightning that night. The sadness, lit up on my father's face with every blue-white strike.

The final memory, the day my father left. I watched from the upstairs window as he placed his suitcase, tools, and a box of Louis L'Amours in the truck bed. He wandered back and forth across the lawn. Then stood in the driveway for a long time while Mother, at the kitchen table with a cup of coffee, pretended to read a newspaper. Finally, my father came in and I heard him plead, "She's just a girl, I should say goodbye to her. At least that." But Mother refused. "You want to go? Then go," she screamed. "We'll get used to it before you shut the door!" I heard her cup smash on the floor, the stark resolution in her voice. And even though I didn't feel the way my mother did, I copied her. Yelled the very same thing from my perch upstairs, the doorway of my tiny bedroom.

I CALL THE LIFE INSURANCE COMPANY but they find no evidence of that policy number. "It's likely been cancelled," the man says. "We purge records on all defunct policies every five years. Sorry."

The document whines as it goes through the shredder. And then everything's quiet.

I lift the cover off Lowen's cage and he shuffles over, opening his beak to reveal a wrinkled tongue the colour of dryer lint. I ignore him. Instead, I think of my father.

I can picture him as he was when I was nine but I can't imagine what he looked like before he died. Can't get a fix on how he must have changed. "Not that I care, but what *were* you doing all this time, Dierk?" I whisper.

Lowen drops to the floor of the cage and begins hitting his head against the bars. After a while, he curls into a ball, making some sort of avian-moaning sound. It's mesmerizing. Then I realize I'm not only wasting time, I'm also late for my appointment with the realtor. I grab my jacket and purse, scoop up all the documents. As I'm racing for the door, I hear Lowen's voice again.

"Goodbye?" he says, quietly. "Goodbye?"

The idiocy of it makes me laugh. "Get used to it," I tell him. And I exit the soon-to-be-on-the-market house.

"Helloo-oo!" Rita calls from the other side of the fence. She's watering a flower bed with one of those long wands, wearing a chili-pepper muumuu and sunglasses big enough to shield the space shuttle during re-entry. "How are you coping, dear? Anything I can do?"

"Everything's under control. Just late for an appointment."

"Oh, well. Off you go, then." She gestures towards the car with the sprinkler.

"Actually Rita, I do have a question."

"Yes?"

"Do you know someone named Eva? Connected to my father, I mean?"

She takes off her huge glasses and taps them on her chest, thinking. "No, Deary. No one I remember," she says. Then she picks an orange pansy from the tray of flowers she's about to plant and shows it to me. I nod, though everything about the flower, the yard, her garden, is completely unremarkable.

When she reaches for another, I cut her off. "Do you recall seeing any guests over here? Maybe someone you didn't know?"

"No, no. Nothing like that. Dierk kept to himself for the most part. Other than Lowen, your father was pretty much alone the five years I've been here. Strange, isn't it? You don't suppose he actually liked being alone, do you?"

THE REALTOR IS A GUY NAMED STEPHEN with obviously dyed hair who also knows nothing about my father. He's more than happy to take on the job of selling the house though. I sign a contract instructing him to put it on the market at whatever price he sees fit. A realtor's dream. *Sell the house. Take the first offer. No haggling, just get rid of it.* Clients like me don't come around very often and Stephen smiles so enthusiastically I can count every single filling in his mouth.

"Shouldn't take long," he tells me as we finish things up. "People are always looking for a good starter place." He guides me towards the door and hands me a folder of documents with his business card stapled to the front. "It's a difficult business, selling a relative's home. Lots of hidden emotion. Lots of worry. But I'm here to help in any way I can. My motto: *Let Stephen be your stress-sponge*," he says.

The first thing that comes to mind—other than that's a stupid motto—is asking him if he knows anyone in town named Eva. But saying that over and over is starting to sound a little birdbrained. So to speak.

"That'll be all, thank you." And then as a joke, I add, "Unless of course you want to adopt a parrot."

"Oh," he replies. "That's a tough one. How's it doing?"

"I don't know, it's a bird. What do you mean?"

"My aunt had a parrot years ago and they're sort of in it for life. When she died, her bird started freaking out, wouldn't eat, kept chewing at himself," he says. "As I recall, the parrot only lasted a couple of months before he expired too. Vet said the animal just couldn't figure out how to handle grief."

I feel my body vibrate and the space between us go cold. Then Stephen gets fidgety like he just realized he's on the verge of losing his commission. Which he is.

"But hey, I'm only a small-town realtor," he says, patting me on the back. "What the hell do I know about these things?"

I'm anxious as I head back to my father's house even though Stephen, as he rightfully implied, was way off base. His aunt was a million years old and her parrot more likely died from second-hand smoke or eating its dinner off Styrofoam meat trays than anything else. That's the bottom line here and it's what I tell myself the entire drive. Lowen—even though I don't care one way or the other—will thrive in the end, living a happy, fruitful, meaningful life. Whether he deserves it or not.

When I get there, I stumble out of the car and drop the realtor's booklet in the driveway. Thankfully, Rita's not in her yard this time, waving her big hand and *helloo-oo-ing* me all the way to the nuthouse. I gather everything up, and enter the house.

The phone rings as soon as I get inside, making my heart pound again. "Who's calling please?" I ask.

"Oh, hi. I'm just inquiring about your ad, about the African Grey," the voice says.

"Yes?"

"Well, I wonder if I could see him. Is there a good time?"

Lowen's lying on the floor of the cage, his head resting on a patchy outstretched wing. He's motionless, stiff-looking. It doesn't really seem like he's breathing anymore.

"I'm sorry," I tell the man on the phone. "The bird's been sold."

"Oh, that's too bad. I was hoping..."

I hang up and drop the phone on the table. Then I stand there for a while and tell myself *it's not my fault, it's not my fault.* When I can't take it any longer, I walk over to the cage and begin tapping on the bars. Once. Twice. Six times. Finally, Lowen lifts his head. And I release the breath I didn't know I was holding.

As soon as my face gets close to the cage, Lowen stands and walks towards me, seemingly okay again. I'm relieved but then angry, like someone just pulled a fast one. Like I'm being led to an ultimate failure. And for some reason, even though it's crazy, I get the impression this whole episode—the sick bird, Rita the judgemental neighbour, the life insurance debacle, maybe even my father's death itself—is the fault of one person and one person only. Eva, the deceitful, behind-the-scenes, stay-in-the-shadows conjuror.

"Okay bird," I say. "No more games."

He closes one eye.

"Tell me, *who's Eva?*"

He climbs up the cage, sits on his wooden bar.

"Eva and Dierk." I say slowly. "E-v-a and D-i-e-r-k."

Nothing.

"Eva. Eva. *Eva*," I say, trying to keep my voice at a non-frictional level.

Finally, he reacts. "Beautiful," he tells me, softly. "My beautiful, beautiful girl."

I close my eyes. Not only do I hear my father's voice but I see him, the physical words spilling from his lips. I feel his fingers on my cheek, smell the tobacco in his shirt. I picture it all and for some reason it stings.

Out of the blue I say, "I'm Elena, Dierk's daughter. Is that who you mean?"

Lowen stares back, vacantly, like I don't exist to him at all. And suddenly I feel very stupid.

What am I doing? He's just an animal, a parrot, *a mimic* for Christ's sake. He doesn't give answers, he does impersonations. Another thing comes to mind: the realization I haven't yet visited the cemetery. Like that has any relevance here at all.

"You think I care?" I yell through the bars, holding the cage like I'm about to shake it. "I don't want your charity, I want a name. Goddamn it, Eva, what is your last name?"

Then it hits me.

I run to the laptop and type in *Werden, Eva*. I refine the search with my father's name and, on a hunch, I add *announcements*.

In the archives of the local paper I find:

Eva Werden (née Cooper) entered into rest suddenly at Merritt, BC on Tuesday, July 11th, 2006. She leaves behind a loving and devoted husband, Dierk Werden, and brother, Jake Cooper of Auckland, New Zealand. Funeral services will be held Saturday, 2:15, at The Church of St Nicholas. She will be dearly missed and never forgotten.

"Got you," I say.

Inexplicably, tears run down my cheeks. It's hard to breathe, my shoulders actually shudder with the force. And my stomach, my heart, every inch of me, feels like a towel that had been twisted for a long time and has now, suddenly, been released.

"My God, get it together, Elena." I wipe my face, hard. "This is none of your business. You have your own life and this is just another irrelevancy in it. Move on. Get it together. You'll get used to it soon enough."

The second I stop talking, Lowen says something as well. Mumbling some phrase over and over. I don't know why but I walk up to the cage, open the door, and put my hand inside. Right next to Lowen.

At first he just sits there, snapping his beak like a pair of shears, making me nervous. But then, bit by bit, he sidles over and steps up onto my wrist. He's heavier than I imagined, his grip tight on my arm. I lift him out of the cage and bring him close to my ear. I feel the heat of his breath on my skin. His beak, smooth and dense.

He starts to speak.

"Got you," he whispers.

"What? I... I don't..."

"Get it together, Elena," he goes on. "Get used to it. Get it together. Get used to it."

The words are clear, very plain. But it's not my father's voice I hear. *It's mine.* He's using my voice now. Except his version is all wrong. His version sounds desperate and bitter and lonely.

I kneel on the carpet and Lowen hops off my arm, walks a few feet away. He's at my father's chair now, standing beside the empty seat, tilting his head from side to side. Everything around us is quiet but it doesn't feel particularly peaceful, it feels like being smothered. All I want to do is pick Lowen up again, feel his warmth, breathe the same air he's breathing, have an actual conversation.

But that doesn't make sense. None of it makes sense.

Lowen flaps his wings and turns away from the chair. He takes a single step towards me, the two of us, face to face.

"Say something," I whisper, holding my hands out towards him. "Please. Please. Say something else."

MR. MONEY-MAKER

"IT'S NO GOOD FORCING IT," Rubin says, a response to Joel's, *Just wake him and get it over with*. It's the reason Rubin stopped taking payment upfront in the first place, people got fidgety, afraid the dog might snooze through the whole visit and they'd be out a few bucks, no answer to show for it. And although Rubin doesn't care about someone else's anxiety—life's not fair to us all—it pisses him off that so many regard him as someone who wouldn't refund their money if they asked him to. As if he's the bad guy in all this and not the real, honest-to-goodness victim.

"You know, it's the wife who's worried, not me," Joel says. "To be clear."

"Of course," Rubin agrees, though that's the largest pile of horseshit he's ever heard. *Everybody* wants to know, especially in this town, the carcinogenic time bomb. The dog's the only one in this whole operation who's ever truly unconcerned, lying on the rug like a mound of dough, the pads on his feet pink as a newborn's lung.

Joel works at the mine just like everybody else. (Everybody that is except Rubin.) He came in today at the end of his shift, been here long enough now to have gone through a full pack of gum. Earlier, Rubin made some instant coffee and discussed regional sports, the weather, everything they might have in common. He even brought out some samples of his handmade apple-branch necklaces at which time Joel smiled and said, "I don't think so." If things don't happen soon Joel's bound to give up and go back to his cushy, benefit-laden job wondering what, if anything, grows inside him. And the worst part in all that: Rubin wouldn't get jack for his efforts.

When Joel's wife, Lara, came in last week, the dog didn't act like the frozen turd he's being now. And after it was over Lara smiled and hugged Rubin like he was a superhero, like he'd performed some small-town miracle. It was nice, but if he actually could perform miracles—nothing against Joel's wife—but if he could, he sure as hell wouldn't waste it on anyone except himself.

"More coffee?" Rubin offers.

Joel stares at Rubin's hands reaching for the mug, all his missing fingers. There's a flash of sympathy on his face or maybe revulsion. Either one is par for the course. "Sorry," he says. "I didn't mean to..."

Before Mr. Inconsiderate can say or do anything else remarkably stupid, there's a scuffling noise behind them. Rubin doesn't have to look to know what it is. The dog, stretching. "He's awake," he tells Joel.

The animal's hindquarters extend into the air, his claws dig deep into the carpet. He shakes each leg separately then stands there, solemn as a minister. Rubin makes him sit and, strictly for show, gives him some baseball-style hand signals. The dog faces Joel. He takes three or four long sniffs, walks into the other room and lies down on the futon couch.

"All right. Pay up," Rubin says, holding out his hand. "You're clear."

THE DOG MIGHT HAVE BEEN BORN with it for all Rubin knows. A scruffy, genetic misfit. He first came upon him at the scrapyard while scrounging for jewellery wire and other useable crap. They approached each other slowly, flanked by a smouldering mound of plastic and the skeleton of a minivan. The animal looked pathetic; his fur riddled with ticks and spear grass, tattered and filthy as a rug. He seemed vaguely sarcastic if you got right down to it with his perpetually upturned lip, his distant, smoky gaze. Despite all that, there was something about him Rubin liked, something he couldn't explain. He checked the dog's tail to assess his friendliness but there wasn't one. It'd been cropped away or broken or maybe even blown right off at the ass. Hardly a discernible stub left in its place. How in all honesty could Rubin *not* have taken an animal like that home with him?

The dog gets up, moseys over to his food dish and waits. He doesn't fuss. Doesn't get excited. Doesn't even groom himself. And if Rubin decided not to fill his bowl today, he wouldn't scratch or bark. He'd wander off and go back to sleep. The perfect pet, remote and distant as an emperor penguin.

The first diagnosis occurred in April. The town was in the middle of a civic election and Sarah Newson, the incumbent mayor, came glad-handing door to door. Initially, Rubin wasn't sure if he should invite her in or what. Who knew the protocol for that sort of thing? The number of hassles it might lead to?

"Are you a decided voter, Mr. Tack?" the mayor said from the hallway. Her requisite smile had no oomph at all, like she was exhausted with Rubin already and knew he hadn't voted in any election, ever, in his entire life. In actuality there was a tumour the size of an eyeball in her left breast sucking the energy right out of her. Something neither one of them had a clue about at the time.

Before Rubin could answer, the dog started circling the mayor. He licked her blouse when she leaned down, pressed his nose into her chest hitting the tumour, painfully, dead on. Two weeks later she returned with the doctor's report. Two weeks after that, a full page article in the local paper and a bit piece in the nationals. And now, three confirmed positives later, people even come from down in the valley for a scan. Go figure.

The phone rings and Rubin fumbles with the receiver; his hands, tired from feeding branch segments through the bead borer. Worth answering though. If the caller's a customer, it'd be the third this week and at twenty-five bucks a scan, that's not bad.

"Hello?" he says, trying not to sound impatient.

"Is this Rubin Tack?"

"Tack-fully so."

"My name's Caleb. I work for *The Oprah Winfrey Show*, guest acquisition department. Do you have a minute?"

WHEN RUBIN WAS A CHILD, his mother used to bring him to the backyard on warm summer nights. She'd put a blanket on the grass, an ashtray for herself, and they'd lie there looking for comets. She said he was a shooting star in his own right and like a giant idiot he believed her. "You're destined to do big things in life, Rubin. Good things. Things that really matter," she told him, sucking on a filtered Cameo.

He holds his hands in front of him now—just a thumb and two fingers remaining on each one. Not even a knuckle to show where the others were before the accident. When he's beading, or doing anything really, they look more like beetle mouths than hands. If that's the destiny his mother was talking about, she could have it.

Truth is Rubin wasn't looking to do much of anything, special or otherwise. He was waiting for something to happen *to him*. This is how he figured it'd play out: the mine (that never hired him) spewed out all kinds of despicable pollution—the tailings pond near the well, the big, phallic smokestacks—so it was only a matter of time before diseases started popping up like maggots. And Rubin lived right on the edge of town, closest to the mine site. Sooner or later he'd find some lump in his neck, blood in his urine, a sore that wouldn't heal. And then, lawsuit money.

But now, instead of all that, Oprah wants him as her guest on TV and two things immediately come to mind. One, Oprah sure beats chemotherapy. And two, it's about bloody time.

In six weeks Rubin and the dog will fly to Chicago, stay at a fancy hotel, eat good, paid-for meals. And though he only gets a small honorarium for his trouble, this kind of thing opens doors. The chance he's been waiting for. He doesn't want to use the term *meal ticket*, but hey, whatever.

He pushes a chair onto the sandy, rutted porch outside his home. Carefully, he lifts the sign he just painted above the door and nails it in place. *Cancer Scans by Oprah-Dog—$150.*

RUBIN SITS BESIDE THE DOG and pets him, smoothing out the imperfections in his fur. Dozens of scars run across his back like tiny bits of scrap metal wedged beneath the skin. They feel, for all intents and purposes, like whip marks. And then there's that damn lost tail and whatever story's behind that. This dog's had a hard life, no doubt about it. Exactly like Rubin's own lousy existence.

He was twelve when the accident happened, the day before Hallowe'en. Grayson, a friend from school, had a brother old enough to buy fireworks and the three of them raced out onto the soccer field with a full bag. *Cluster Bombs, Phantom Blasts,* a boxy thing named *Godzilla.* The first few went off perfectly and then Rubin lit a huge barrage, *The Dream Weaver.* It tilted and he tried to straighten it before ignition. He doesn't remember anything after that except the sound. Horse hooves on pavement, trees falling, pumpkins being dropped from way, way up. And then silence.

There were many people at fault that night, none of them Rubin. He was twelve, as incapable of blame as the dog lying in front of him now. But Grayson's brother, Christ, an eighteen year old! And Grayson's parents need to take responsibility for being such unaware slobs. The town council too, for hemming and hawing over a proposed fireworks ban. The fireworks company itself. The list goes on and on.

Now Rubin lives a life where everyone pities him—rightfully so—but that's the extent of their generosity. When he thinks about that, the injustice of everything, he gets so furious there's just about no amount of money that could settle him down.

Someone knocks on the door. He feels the softness of the dog's ears between his fingers, and goes to answer.

Dwight Kingsley from the mine, the putz in human resources who interviewed Rubin years ago for the job he didn't get. He never said why they passed on him but it's not as if he had to.

"Hi Rubin." He removes his sunglasses and puts them in a small cloth bag. "How are you these days?"

"A-OK," Rubin answers, making an OK sign with his remaining fingers. It amounts to a circle and an extended middle finger pointed right at Dwight's nose.

Dwight nods. He's wearing a brown leather coat, the ultrasoft kind that costs an arm. If Rubin could, he'd pull it over Mr. Discrimination's head, spin him around, and boot his ass right out the door. Unless he came here looking for a scan, of course. Rubin should probably find that out first.

"I don't want to take up too much of your time but I hear you're going to be on TV soon," Dwight says. "Congratulations."

"Is that why you came? Congratulations?"

"No, not really. Look, I know how you feel about the company, Rubin," Dwight goes on. "But nobody likes bad publicity, especially the televised kind."

"I'm going on the show. You can't stop me."

"On the contrary. I want you to go. You can represent us in a sense. Preserve our good environmental name."

Rubin pauses, letting this bizarre conversation sink in. "What's in it for me?" he says finally. "I mean, financially?"

THERE HASN'T BEEN A POSITIVE SCAN since the new sign went up but business has been great anyway. Rubin's even managed to sell some necklaces in the deal, working the souvenir angle of all things. Hell, he might even bring something to hock to Oprah when he goes, maybe the choker with the bullshit whalebone pendant. What a coup that would be! He just about craps his own pants when he thinks about it.

The bottom line, he's made more money in the last few weeks than he did in the previous six months. He has tons saved already, more than a thousand bucks. In fact he's going to use some of it to get the dog an official *Oprah Winfrey* t-shirt at the studio gift shop. Something to wear while he works his lucrative magic.

"That's right, buddy," he says to the dog lounging by the heat vent. "A nice t-shirt, just for you."

Rubin lies on the carpet and rubs his chin against the dog's stubbly nose. Then he says in a voice most people use only for babies, "You and me Mr. Money-Maker, we're going places. Uh huh. Yes we are."

The dog leans into him, rests his head on Rubin's arm and closes his eyes. Rubin closes his too but the moment ends with a knock on the door. "Duty calls," he says as he heads for the entrance.

The woman standing there is new to him. She's young, nineteen maybe, and tiny. Her hair's tied back in a ponytail and although it's not cold outside she's wearing a wool vest. He also notices some homemade jewellery. Glass beads on a thick leather string, silver rings, a bent copper bracelet polished orange, the colour of a comet's tail.

She takes a clipboard from under her arm and Rubin frowns.

"Don't worry, I'm super-low pressure," she says. "It's just a petition to prompt the mine into cleaning up its environmental act. Slam-dunk, actually, almost signs itself." She winks at him and smiles.

Rubin examines the clipboard, and laughs out loud.

If this is a joke it's really quite good. All these years nobody cared. And now, a petition! If she'd got to him last week he'd have been all over the damn thing. But not anymore.

When Dwight visited Rubin, he brought a folder full of studies the mine conducted on its ecological impact. Rubin leafed through them but mostly he just read the factsheet Dwight wants him to reference on the talk show. Statistics like the cancer rates in town being the same as everywhere else in the province, the giant amount of money the company has spent on reclamation and tailings treatment, and the mine's own water results, testing out as clean and drinkable as a mountain stream. "Our water's even fluoridated," he told Rubin, "for your teeth."

The funny part is he wasn't going to trash the mine on Oprah anyway, too busy promoting his own ends. But now, by some strange twist of Karma, the mine's giving him a whack of cash not to say things he wasn't going to say in the first place. How fucked up is that?

"I don't think so," he says to the girl at the door. "Our air is fine, our water is fine."

And because he's feeling smug he goes over to the sink, pours a glass and takes a big, exaggerated drink. He dumps the rest of it into the dish on the floor beside him.

The dog moseys over and laps at the bowl.

"You're funny," the girl says. "But like I said, low pressure. Hey pupper. How about you? Will you put your paw print here?" She puts her clipboard on the floor so she can pet him. "So you're the famous dog, huh?"

"Would you like him to scan you?"

"Me? No thanks. I wouldn't want to know my fortune ahead of time. Screw up all my plans."

Rubin doesn't respond.

"It's a big responsibility," she goes on, patting the animal's head. "Taking care of someone who can't take care of himself."

Rubin's suddenly uncomfortable with the path this conversation has taken. Mostly because his fingers are sore and there's no money to be had here. But also because he's not sure if the clipboard girl is talking to him now or if she's still talking to the goddamn dog.

THE ONLY SUITCASE RUBIN HAS is a heavy, orange thing that smells like a bus depot. The latch barely closes and there are no wheels which means it's probably from the fifties. It was his mother's luggage and it annoys him he's thinking of her now, the day of his big flight. If she were still around, would she be happy for him? Is being on Oprah *shooting star* enough? It'll lead to a pocket full of money and that's more than sufficient for a sad sack like Rubin. No matter what anyone, including his mother, might think.

He turns to the dog. "What would you wear on TV if you were me? Hmm?"

The dog doesn't move but his eyes follow Rubin around the room while he packs. Rubin gave him a bath last night using his own personal shampoo and right now they both smell like apricots.

He grabs the nicest thing he has from the closet—wool jacket, white button-up shirt, and a pair of black pants—the outfit he wore for his predetermined interview, the no-thank-you event with Dwight Kingsley. It's suitable for the occasion or completely jinxed, only one way to find out. He puts it in the suitcase and fumbles the latch closed. In a separate bag he packs some dog food, a blanket, and the new chew toy he got on sale at the drugstore; the woman from the airline suggested bringing a few of the animal's favourite things for the long flight. "It's noisy and dark in the cargo hold. Something familiar in the crate will keep him calm," she said. "Everybody likes calm."

When he's finished packing he takes an ice pack and puts it on his finger-stubs to soothe the phantom pains he still gets after all these years. Then he wraps a second ice pack in a tea towel and places it where the dog's tail should be. They stay nestled like that for a while, leaning into each other until the airport shuttle van pulls up and honks for them to come out.

INSIDE THE TERMINAL, dozens of travellers wheel their suitcases around effortlessly while Rubin struggles with his. He shifts the case from side to side and searches for a luggage cart; of course, none are available. He puts the suitcase down and checks his ticket. It isn't clearly marked which way to go and Rubin hasn't exactly spent much time in an airport before. He looks at the boarding pass, at the many numbered signs around the building. The dog sits quietly beside him the whole time.

"Can I help you?" someone asks.

A woman in an airport uniform. Her face is hard, stippled like the skin of a lemon, and her hair's tied back in a bun high on the top of her head. Rubin hands her his ticket. She takes it and glances at the dog. Then she looks at Rubin like he just presented her with a bowl of ass hair.

"Is the animal travelling too?" she says.

"Yes."

"Did you preregister?"

"Yes."

"Follow me."

Rubin walks behind her, suppressing the urge to trip her with the dog's leash. The only reason he doesn't say something like, *Excuse me, I think you forgot to go fuck yourself this morning*, is because this woman is a key to unlocking Rubin's windfall. His wallet feels fatter with every step and nothing, not even Miss Lemon-Face here, will spoil his mood.

They veer off the path of the other travellers and end up down a long, windowless hallway. A cleaning man leans against the wall, holding a mop as grey and unkempt as his beard. He doesn't say a word as they pass, but scrutinizes the dog the whole way.

"In here," the woman says. She goes into an elevator at the end of the hall. Rubin puts his suitcase down and stands beside her. The dog leans into his leg.

"Has the dog flown before?"

"No," Rubin says. "I don't think so."

The doors open into what looks like a high school basement. Bare cement floors, drain hole in the middle of the room, a puzzle of air ducts and water pipes across the ceiling. And along the far wall, a row of plastic dog-cages, each with a small, barred window so the animals can see.

"We can take it from here," the woman says.

A man approaches wearing work gloves and overalls. He looks more like a plumber than an animal handler. The woman takes Rubin's blanket and puts it in one of the cages. She tosses in the chew toy. The man reaches for the leash.

"Here we go," Rubin says.

The dog stands before the kennel. For the first time ever the fur on the scruff of his neck stands up, stiff and bristly as a toilet brush. Rubin tries to smooth it down but it bounces right back. The flesh underneath quivers and the dog's lip flares, revealing yellow teeth and dark, pigmented gums.

He barks, sharply.

"Bad dog," Rubin says. It's a stupid thing to say but he wasn't prepared for this. The dog's never barked before. Not once.

"You'll be fine. These people will take care of you."

He barks again. Four or five times with deep, low growls in between.

The man tugs his gloves tighter and rubs the leather palms together. "It's best if we do it," he says. "Seriously."

The dog pulls on his leash, tries to wiggle free of his collar. His eyes are huge and his whole body, shaking.

Rubin bends down and whispers in his ear. "Hey pal," he says. "Don't screw it up okay? There's nothing to worry about." He pets him with his spent hands. Rubs his coat all over, trying to stop the animal from shuddering. Trying to make this work. Then, through the fur, Rubin feels something he's never noticed before. A lump. The exact size, texture and hardness of a walnut shell.

The dog twists around and tries to lick that spot. He can't reach it though, so he turns and growls at the airport staff again.

Rubin presses his fingers into his temples. He pictures a sack of money, so big he has to kneel down and wiggle his arms underneath to move it. It's right there in front of him. Right friggin' there. "We'll fix you up later," he says to the dog. "Don't worry. You'll be fine."

"That's right," the plumber-man says. "He'll be fine." He reaches for the leash again. Rubin hesitates, then gives it to him and walks away.

Behind him he hears the dog bark, his claws dragging across the cement floor. A yip. A strained cough from the pull of his collar. Another yip. Rubin fakes a coughing fit of his own to drown out the struggle. He still hears it though, all of it, until he gets into the hallway and closes the door behind him.

RUBIN FEELS LIKE HE'S BEING WATCHED as he walks through first class. The rich folk are all assessing his hands or his second-hand clothes, making him feel like a thief. Even after he takes his seat with the regular people he feels scrutinized. Dissected even. The whole thing playing out much crappier than it's supposed to.

He flags down a stewardess. A young, plain-looking woman with big cheeks and freckles all over her face. He chooses her because she seems friendliest. "Excuse me," he says. "Can I get something to drink?"

"You sure can. But not until we're up there." She points skyward.

"Oh. Right," Rubin says. He turns to the window beside him. A man on the tarmac drives a luggage cart in a meaningless circle, a dog-crate piled haphazardly among the baggage. But it's not his. The cart drives off the other way, manoeuvres between two smaller planes, and disappears.

He'll get the dog checked the second they get back. And he'll find the best people to do it too. Not some crappy horse doctor but someone who knows this kind of thing, a top of the line specialist. There's nothing to worry about, at least nothing substantial enough to kibosh the Oprah Winfrey gravy train.

He hears a noise, a torque-wrench or a compressor squealing. It's loud inside the cabin and must be much louder underneath him in the cargo hold. The wrench stops and he hears something else, faint but there. A raspy, persistent barking in the belly of the aircraft. He puts the airline headphones over his ears, but there's no sound yet so he stuffs them back into the seat pocket in front of him.

Barking doesn't mean anything in particular. It's what dogs do. Besides, they'll only be gone a week. Nobody dies of a tumour in a week. The dog will be fine until they get back home. Absolutely, perfectly fine.

As long as his heart doesn't give out in the cargo hold.

He leans forward and puts his hands over his face.

"Excuse me I think you're in my seat," someone says. "Oh, it's you. Hello again."

A woman in the aisle wearing a glass bead necklace, copper bracelet, wool vest. The petition girl. Right here in front of him as conspicuous as an albatross.

"This is a funny coincidence, isn't it?" she says. "Life's too weird sometimes. How's your pupper by the way?"

"You've got to be kidding me."

"I'm sorry?"

Rubin turns to the window again, an image of the dog's face in the glass. Those eyes, looking right into him. Reflecting the life they've both had. And even though it's like finding a pot of gold at the end of the rainbow, then pissing on it and setting it on fire…

He stands up and squeezes by the woman. "Seat's all yours," he says.

She points at her ticket in explanation but Rubin couldn't care less. The flight takes off soon, he doesn't have much time. He runs up the aisle, bangs his knee on one of the armrests, and continues into first class, the section he should have been enjoying all along if life were fair at all. He gets stuck behind some snub-nose standing up like he owns the airline, taking off his thousand-dollar jacket. Rubin waits for two or three seconds, and then pushes him out of the way. He rushes up to the stewardess at the front, the one with the pleasant face.

"I have to get off the plane," he says.

"I'm sorry. You're too late. They're about to close up."

Another woman turns a big handle on the cabin door, sealing it shut while the rest of the crew prepare their useless pre-flight safety speech. And then, right on cue, the seatbelt sign chimes, flashing for him to sit down.

It's finished. He missed his chance.

People wait for him to settle in his seat. He turns, slowly, and starts walking towards his row. Halfway there, he stops. The dog is barking below him again, more and more frantic with each yelp.

He takes a deep breath and looks at the ceiling. "Is there no one else on earth," he whispers, "that you can fuck with besides me?"

He returns to the front of the plane, to the stewardess, and holds his hands in the air for her—for everyone—to see. "Is it because I'm handicapped? Is that what you're saying?" he says in a loud voice, full of phoney disbelief. "Is this what they call *discrimination?*"

"I don't know what you're talking about," the stewardess says. Her face pales. She turns to the cabin crew behind her who've stopped to listen; the entire front section of the airplane, hushed.

Rubin leans in and whispers, "Look, I work for *The Oprah Winfrey Show*, okay." He flashes the logo on his *Special Visitor* lanyard. "And I know neither you nor the airline wants any bad publicity here."

"Of course not," the stewardess says. "But..."

"No buts." Rubin positions a hand in front of her face to stop her sentence. He wiggles his remaining fingers, and knows he's got her.

"Here's the deal," he says, "I don't want a refund. I don't want compensation. All I want is to get my dog out of that crate and go home. Now, are you going to tell me that's too much to ask for? Seriously, to my face? Is that what you're about to tell me?"

She turns to her coworkers again and, in near-unison, they nod.

Miss Friendly escorts him off the plane, through the jet bridge, and back inside the terminal. After discussing things with the supervisor who checked Rubin's passport on the way in, she says, "I'm very sorry for any misunderstanding or personal inconvenience you may have experienced, Mr. Tack. Our customers—you—deserve the best. Please accept this apology on behalf of myself, the crew, and the entire airline."

Rubin pauses, letting this small, soothing victory wash over him. "Apology Tack-fully accepted," he says. Then he sits in the elite passenger zone to wait, sipping a complimentary coffee and watching the crew reopen the cargo hold, locate his luggage, and deliver his dog to his side.

THE SUPPORT GROUP

"WELL?" MARILYN SAYS, handing Eric the lists she's been working on. One, a number of hors d'oeuvres she wants to prepare after their son goes out; the other, details of the parents who'll be attending, their children's names written in brackets as descriptors. Three couples will join them in tonight's endeavour, perfect for the initial meeting. It's a number that shouldn't overwhelm Eric anyway and that's worth its weight in something.

"I think it's… it seems great," Eric says, giving her an exaggerated thumbs-up.

When Marilyn first told her husband the idea he joked about it of course, his way of handling everything he doesn't like. "Sounds awesome," he told her. "Angry parents waving bludgeons in the air. You, at the front, urging them on." Then he proceeded to act out the scene in an admittedly decent Churchill accent, smacking the counter with an umbrella and smoking an invisible cigar. Marilyn laughed at first and then immediately cursed herself. The last thing she wanted was to encourage him.

"Have you decided what you're going to wear?"

"Ah, yes. The battle garb."

She ignores the bait. "I think we should start the evening with a roundtable introduction. The only couple we know is Lisa and Vince and I want this to feel like a retreat, a place where people can talk freely. It would be nice if everyone participated."

"Sure would."

"I mean it, Eric. *Everyone.*"

He nods and scratches his chin. In theory, he's being supportive, something other wives would be jealous of. But it's also true she's alone in this while he sits there, oblivious. Listening but not really listening, repeating what she wants him to say. Being very good at pretending.

Paul stomps down the stairs, cutting off her thoughts. She hides the guest list as he enters the kitchen. "Where are you going tonight, sweetie?" she asks.

"Downtown, maybe. I don't know." Paul grabs some food from the fridge, hardly slowing down to flip his bangs out of his eyes.

"Your plans?"

"Mom, we don't make plans. We just *do things.*" He stuffs an apple in his pocket and puts on his shoes. "I'll see you later, though," he says, slamming the door behind him, predictably.

Marilyn grips the edge of the counter until her fingers blanch. Eric, beside her, is nodding already, pre-emptively agreeing with whatever she might think.

"Do you see," she begins, suddenly so frustrated she has to fight back tears, "why this is so important?"

PAUL LIFTS A STONE from the rock wall outside, liberating his package of cigarettes. If his parents knew he smoked, even though it's hardly ever, they'd freak. They'd yell at him at first, like normal parents, but then his mom would want to *analyze the situation, get to the root of the problem.* And his dad would stand beside her, agreeing and shaking his head like someone just died instead of smoked. That's not an exaggeration either. Paul's life. He can hardly blame his friends for crapping all over him about it.

But right now at least he has something better to think

about. As soon as he gets downtown, he's meeting Fanta.

It's nothing crazy, but *she* approached *him* and that's a good sign; girls don't generally fall all over themselves for guys like Paul. The last time he even asked a girl out was ages ago, Ashley Winters in gym class, and he failed so incredibly it became a legend. He couldn't even speak. Mumbling like he had a mouthful of bees or just had his wisdom teeth pulled. She finally asked him, "Are you okay, Paul? Have you been in a fight or something?"

My God. All he could do was walk away at that point. And now, a year later, Jake Pittman still says, "Have you been in a fight or something?" whenever Paul even thinks about talking to a girl. There's no way to forget about it, ever. It's become a thing.

Pitty loves stuff like that, stuff that makes other people look stupider than him. He's the guy who invented *spit-war* and *the shiner game* and he wears t-shirts with the word "fuck" hidden inside Chinese symbols. Paul only calls him friend because to call him anything else means you've opened yourself up for a crotch-kick or a blindside punch to the head. Who needs that kind of attention?

Paul stops at the end of the driveway, examining the worn-out package of Player's in his hand. *Fanta doesn't smoke!*

In fact, he's seen her make faces when other people light up, squinting and waving her hands back and forth to clear the air. "Right out of the gate, Paul," he whispers. "Almost, almost." He turns around and stashes the smokes under the rock again. He doesn't even like cigarettes anyway, kind of funny when you think about it.

That's exactly what he needs to do. *Think!* If he does that, he'll be fine. If he takes things slow, doesn't talk a lot, nods at what Fanta has to say, then this whole night could roll out okay. And Paul might be talked about at school as just another normal guy instead of a gigantic ass-wipe. What a change to the program that would be.

"WELCOME," ERIC SAYS. It's Lisa and Vince from next door. Eric hugs Lisa and shrugs his shoulders apologetically at Vince. The night has just begun and already he feels like he should buy them a box of donuts or one of those balloons that say, *Forgive Me?* If this were a normal Friday evening, Eric would be sitting in front of the TV with a bowl of ice cream softened from the microwave. Vince too, probably, at his own place, in his own favourite chair. But there's nothing like that on the agenda tonight. Tonight—as Marilyn put it—they're *socializing with purpose.*

"Follow me," Eric says. "It's started."

He leads them to the living room where Marilyn has arranged the seats into a semicircle. The table in the middle holds a tray of crackers, a red pepper dip, and some wrinkled black olives that look far too much like deer pellets for Eric's liking. There's a pitcher of fruit juice on the console, some bottled water, a rarely-used ice bucket. And sitting there like they're all in detention together, a group of people Eric has nothing in common with.

But if this is what it takes to keep Marilyn's head above water, this is what they'll do. After all, happy wife, happy life. Something like that.

"Vince, Lisa. I'm so glad you could come," Marilyn says. She guides the neighbours to their place and begins the introductions.

Tim and Joan live in the house on the corner. Eric's seen them before from a distance, gardening like it's the Olympics and doing all the home maintenance projects he should do more of himself. They're a funny couple, both speaking in the same sleepy monotone and wearing nearly-identical glasses—thin wiry things that remind Eric of the scientist on *The Muppet Show* from when Paul was a kid and a night like this, inconceivable.

The other couple, Kip and Christine, own the big stone house a few blocks over. Kip's hair hangs past his shoulders and he's wearing a white t-shirt, a number of thin metal bracelets on each wrist. If Kip hadn't already said he was an accountant, Eric would have pegged him as a musician living in one of those camper vans, a special shelf to hold his bong collection. Christine fits the mould too. Flowery dress, beaded hair, and silver rings on her toes that catch the light whenever she crosses and uncrosses her legs.

Then there's Vince and Lisa, the neighbours who usually come over for things like barbeques instead of this. Lisa's pretty quiet but when she and Marilyn get wound up their conversations can go on for ages, long after Vince and Eric have run out of things to say. That's fine with them though. They're happy to sip beer in peace while the discussion continues around them. Watching heat rise off the concrete patio, ants walking along the edge of the grass. Life, happening.

"So now that we're all acquainted, why don't we jump in?" Marilyn says. "What's wrong with our teenagers? Who'd like to go first?"

The room goes silent as though Marilyn just asked the group for a stool sample. And Eric knows—God how he knows—it's his job to help her out.

Being married is like living in a rowboat. One person gives orders while the other bails endlessly. He knows his role in the operation and he's fine with that arrangement. In fact, he's fine with most things in life and can't remember the last time he had a serious problem with anything, ever. Not unless Marilyn brought it up first.

Just as he's about to break the silence, Kip puts his hand up. "I don't know if it's appropriate," he says, "but we've brought some wine." He lifts a bottle from the bag at his feet. "Sometimes it's easier to talk while sharing a cup of vino."

Eric knows Marilyn's lips are doing that weird thing they do when she can't say what she wants to say; he doesn't need to look.

"To grease the wheels," Kip goes on, his bracelets jingling as he tilts the bottle back and forth.

"Well," Marilyn begins, "I suppose..."

Eric shrugs in a *what else can we do?* sort of way. Then he goes to get some glasses from the cupboard. He takes the long way around to the kitchen though, so Marilyn can't see the grin on his face. No sense pressing his luck.

PAUL FINDS FANTA STANDING outside *The Brickyard Pizza* and right away his lungs feel like they're wrapped in elastic bands. He calms himself, getting his heart back to normal before walking over. Then he tries to wave and his finger gets caught on a thread in his pocket. It looks like he's having a seizure.

"Hi, Paul," Fanta says. "You good?"

"Good," he answers, managing to free his hand. "How good are you?"

He closes his eyes and thinks about going home.

Fanta smiles and says, "I'm pretty good, I'd say. Care for some pizza?"

"Okay," Paul answers. He forces himself *not* to say anything else as she opens the door and they go inside.

Fanta's pretty tall for a girl and way smarter than anybody else in Grade Ten. She usually says whatever's on her mind too which makes her less popular than she could be. Paul likes that about her though—it means she doesn't hang out with the people who tend to make fun of him on a regular basis. She keeps looking at him after they sit down and he doesn't know what to do with his hands. He folds the menu, waves across the room at someone he doesn't recognize, rubs a black mark off his shoe. Picks at the logo on his napkin.

"Paul?" Fanta says. "I'm over here. It's okay to look at me on a date."

Paul expects to see a scowl on her face, the same look his mother's been giving him lately. Instead, Fanta's grinning and it's not even weird at all. It feels normal, like they've been doing this for months.

After they order, they have a long conversation about bizarre pizza toppings—crickets, fried eggs, smoked reindeer—and as far as he knows, he doesn't screw anything up. When the food arrives he eats slowly, another thing he told himself to do, and wipes his mouth a lot. He laughs at the jokes she makes and not because he's nervous, but because she's funny. When they're done, Fanta reaches over and touches his hand; it feels like someone just stirred his insides with a cattle prod.

"Your name is cool," he says, trying to distract himself from the waves of anxiety in his chest.

"You know my folks named me after a pop, right?"

"I like pop," he says. And instead of laughing, she squeezes his hand. For a second he thinks about putting his other hand on top of hers but that might be sweaty and stupid, so he doesn't.

"They're talking about us tonight, you know," she goes on.

"What?"

"Our parents. They're at your house right now having a meeting about how to handle teenagers. A support group or something."

"Oh my God, I'm sorry," Paul says. "My Mom's like that. She has all kinds of problems, I can't even begin to say... and she's..."

"Hey, don't worry. My folks are into that kind of stuff and besides, they packed a couple bottles of wine."

"Okay," Paul says. He nods like he understands which he completely doesn't.

"So they'll probably be at it a while. Most of the night I expect," she goes on, taking a long, sexy sip from her straw. "And that means neither one of us has to be home anytime soon. Now do we?"

"EXACTLY!" MARILYN SAYS. She makes sure Eric's paying attention, and then focuses on Tim and Joan who have the floor. They've been describing their son, Julian, how he's been removing himself from their lives bit by bit, a kind of reverse pointillism. The similarity between their situations is precisely what Marilyn had hoped for, a confirmation, something more substantial than Eric's usual approach: *Is that what you think, honey? I think that too.* If she has to give credit to a couple glasses of chardonnay for this breakthrough, well, so be it.

"One last thing," Tim says. "Our son won't do his chores anymore."

"And the scowl he gives when we ask... It's un-Godly," Joan adds. They hold hands and take their seats again.

In her peripheral vision, Marilyn sees—or maybe imagines—Eric rolling his eyes.

"Thank you both," she tells them. "Very much."

If it were appropriate, she'd give them a hug right now. One for Lisa and Vince as well, who've just finished discussing their daughter, Chloe. She's been so closed up lately it's like they're "visiting her in prison" when they try to have a conversation. Marilyn feels bad for them, of course. But at the same time, she's overjoyed at the same-boat-ness of it all.

Even Kip and Christine, the couple Marilyn wasn't sure about, shared their difficulties. They employ a pick-your-battles philosophy with their daughter, Fanta, but recently they've had to bite their tongues almost every day. "Slow down, breathe. Take a mental diazepam," was how Christine put it while Kip stood beside her, drinking wine and adding one-line colour commentary. "You know what they say about brains and assertiveness…" And, "Just like when I was a teenager, back when the earth was cooling."

When Marilyn took her turn, she spoke of Paul's attitude, of course. But then she found herself talking about the mistakes she and Eric made over the years, going back to where it all began, when Paul was nine. He wanted to quit his swimming lessons and she and Eric let him. They thought he'd regret it and learn from the experience, the concept of *natural consequences*. But now she knows it was nothing but lazy parenting. Paul didn't think about outcomes, he was nine for God's sake. He used the free time to watch cartoons and the only thing he learned was how to get his own way. That moment, plainly, was the power-shift.

While she spoke, Eric nodded at all the right moments, refilled glasses with the second bottle of wine Kip and Christine brought. Said, "That's right. Uh huh. Of course," going through his typical, *altar-boy motions*. But none of it had any meaning, like everything else in Marilyn's life.

What he really needs to do is contribute something new to the conversation, something significant, something of his own. And yes, right about now would be nice.

"Eric? Would you like to add anything," she prompts, "to close off the first part of the evening?"

"Absolutely," he answers, making the hairs on Marilyn's neck stand up. He clears his throat and begins immediately. "There's not a lot to say that hasn't already been covered. But there is one word I haven't heard tonight, a word I'd use to describe our son more than any other. It's a small word, a powerful one, and it sums up life at our house perfectly."

He pauses to take a sip and Marilyn knows exactly what he's doing: executing comic timing. She's an idiot. And she's just given him an audience.

"What's the word?" Kip asks, playing into Eric's hands perfectly.

"Ah, yes. The word. Well, that word is *loud!*"

He yells it and everyone, except Marilyn, bursts into laughter.

"Our son can turn anything into noise," he says. "He closes cupboard doors with enough force to cut a snake in half, walks around like he's putting out spot fires or auditioning for the army. It's like we're living under a dance studio in a town where all the children have wooden feet."

Eric does a stationary march. He looks into an invisible fridge and slams the door with both hands, kicking it for emphasis.

"Oh my God. That's perfect," Vince says.

"You nailed it," Kip adds.

Before he can go further, Marilyn interrupts, taking the focus off her jackass husband. "Thank you, Eric," she says, more abruptly than needed. "And on that note, I think we could probably all use a little break."

AFTER DINNER, FANTA LEADS PAUL to the park beside the lake. There's a playground with a tire swing, a slide, and a climbing frame Paul fell off once when he was ten, fracturing his arm in two places. The doctor gave him a cast which Paul figured his friends would sign at school the next day. Instead, they held him down while Pitty drew pictures of cartoon penises all over it, complete with stick legs and big smiling faces. He called it the "cast of dicks" and Paul had to practically drench the thing in Liquid Paper before he went home that day.

But now he's walking through that same playground with that same arm wrapped around Fanta's waist. And this is turning out to be the best night of his life so far. No contest.

They stop at the shoreline gazebo where the old people in town like to watch fish jump or fat blue dragonflies sweeping the water like search planes. The lake itself is small and man-made but it gets de-weeded and stocked with rainbow trout every few years by the outdoor society. Right in the middle, there's an aerator—a giant version of the kind you see in aquariums—humming in the dark. To the left, a small beach with a swimming area and an old wooden dock bobbing up and down in the waves like a dead animal.

Fanta pulls a blanket from her bag and lays it out on the gazebo floor. "Shall we sit," she says, "and be civilized?"

"Sounds divine," Paul answers, using an accent that comes off more like *punch-drunk* than the *British* he was going for.

"In keeping with civility..." She lifts a bottle of wine and two plastic glasses from her bag. She hands the corkscrew to Paul and he holds it for a minute, panicked.

The only time he's had anything to drink before was a vodka cooler last year on Canada Day. It tasted like something you'd put in a hummingbird feeder, and when the guys weren't looking he dumped it on the grass.

"We'll do it together," Fanta says, taking Paul's hand and guiding it over the bottle. They clasp fingers and twist the opener into the top. When the cork comes out, Paul points the bottle away, expecting bubbles to spurt out all over the place. Then he realizes it's not that kind of wine.

Fanta doesn't acknowledge his mistake though, and Paul shrugs his shoulders and carries on. He doesn't even mind that she knows he's a total rookie. It feels like he could tell her anything, be an idiot all night and she'd still have the same reassuring glow in her cheeks. What that means exactly, he hasn't figured out. But right now, sitting with her on the blanket... who cares?

"WELL, THAT WAS STUPID," Eric whispers, splashing water on his face in the bathroom. After Marilyn called the recess she disappeared into the kitchen, giving him a look that could have dropped a water buffalo from across a field.

Seemed appropriate in the moment though, trying to lighten things up. The others made it sound like their lives were ending, like they'd been stricken with a plague instead of an adolescent. But being shocked by anything your teenager does is like being surprised when your ass feels wet in the shower. Even Eric knows that and he's not exactly one for contemplation.

As for Paul, he's not a bad kid, not even close. Sure, he talks back a little but he's a teenager. Besides, Eric gets the impression he takes a lot of guff from the guys at school. Letting off steam at home is probably just what he needs right now and in the grand scheme of things, isn't that their job as parents anyway? To be the support group when all else fails?

None of that, however, changes the fact Eric just screwed up and has to apologize to Marilyn for being a jerk. Even if it turns out he's a jerk who's been right about everything all along. *Happy wife, et cetera, et cetera, et cetera.*

He opens the bathroom door and Marilyn's right there, leaning against the wall in the hallway. She doesn't look particularly angry but that's probably a bad thing. They're alone for the moment though, and since this isn't going to get easier later on, now's as good a time as any.

"Hey," he says, touching her arm. "I might have got carried away back there."

Marilyn doesn't react and her silence makes him feel like he's at the bottom of a pool. Finally she says, "Well at least you participated. That's something anyway."

"Really?"

She walks past him into the bathroom. "No, Eric. Not really."

PAUL GIVES HIS EMPTY GLASS to Fanta and she puts it on the bench beside hers. He didn't like the wine but neither did she and that made them both laugh, spilling the rest of the bottle on the gazebo floor. They had fun though, toasting the sunset, the lake, the mosquitoes, and anything else they could think of. Paul also toasted Fanta at the end, saying she looked even prettier outside at night, like stars reflecting on the water. You could have made nachos with the cheese from that line, but she responded with, "I think we should stay out here forever then, because I like what you just said."

In fact, she likes everything he says, and it makes him feel *safe*. A weird word to describe what she does to him but it's exactly the truth. The only other place he feels safe these days is at home, if you can imagine that. Even though his parents are defective, at least they're not pulling for him to fall on his face all the time. Most of his friends, it seems, are just waiting for Paul to shit the bed again, become the next funny line. He doesn't like to compare Fanta to his parents of course, that's completely gross. But *safe* is one word he'd use, as messed up as that might...

Fanta leans in and puts her lips against his; he pulls away, thinking he did something wrong. She takes his hand and places it on her hip. Then she leans him back, carefully, so he's lying on the blanket. He tries to breathe, to stop his heart from exploding and ruining everything. It keeps going though, faster and faster. And then she's on top of him. Kissing him and showing him what to do.

"Well, would you look at that," someone says, breathing heavily in the darkness beyond the gazebo. "Small Paul getting a tutorial in the park."

"I'M SORRY YOU HAD TO SEE THAT," Marilyn says to the women, all of whom have gathered with her in the kitchen. She starts taking the plastic wrap off the next course, a tray of glazed tarts.

"No need to apologize," Lisa says.

"Yeah. Boys will be boys. And *men* will be boys," Christine adds. "Just be happy they're not dialling escort services or selling cocaine from the basement. Honestly, you can't expect much more."

Joan nods. "Tim does that sometimes, too," she says.

"Escorts or cocaine?" Christine points a finger at her. "Girl, you've been holding out on us."

They laugh, even Marilyn, and it's a *relief,* the opposite feeling she gets when Eric makes a joke. It has to do with intention, she realizes. The purpose of his jokes is to make himself look funny, not to make her feel better. That's the difference right there.

She takes a steel bowl out of the freezer and pours heavy cream and sugar into it while the others continue talking. She whips the mixture with a hand blender, watching it stiffen, turning into something solid. When it's done, she spoons it into the ceramic serving dish resting beneath the window.

The men are in the backyard getting some air, standing next to the fence. Eric rubs his temples, his eyebrows. Kneads the back of his neck like he just finished a marathon. Good, Marilyn thinks. She doesn't want to be the type of person who says he deserves it. But he deserves it.

She watches Kip put his arm around Eric and point to Vince and Lisa's house. Then the three of them converge and boost Vince over the top of the fence. He disappears through the backdoor into his house.

Marilyn turns to see if the other women are watching but they've migrated to the living room, taking the pastry trays and cutlery with them. Outside, Vince returns. He passes something over the fence before climbing back across. Another two bottles of wine, one white, one red.

Eric collects the bottles. And Marilyn, her whole body shaking, brings the bowl of whipped cream into the other room.

It's Pitty—of course—standing on the chip path with a scruffy guy Paul's never seen before. They come over and sit on the bench, each holding a bottle of Coke presumably saturated with some vile mix. Then they give each other this sly look like they're part of a secret asshole-club, and Pitty lights a smoke.

"Don't stop on our account," he says. The guy beside him slaps his leg a few times and fake-loads an invisible shotgun.

"Fanta and I were just hanging out, Pitty. That's all."

"Well, something was hanging out I suppose," Pitty says. "Flopping out, peeking out, poking out. Whatever."

The sidekick-guy laughs again, makes an inchworm gesture with his finger. He takes a swig and Paul notices a long scar on his neck, disappearing under the collar of his shirt. He checks to see if Fanta noticed too, but sees something else in her face instead. Disappointment maybe? Frustration? Regret? And suddenly a familiar panic rises inside him like eels coiling around his rib cage.

He points his finger at the two idiots, and—without thinking too much about it—says, "Leave us alone. Okay?"

Pitty stands up immediately, puts his Coke bottle on the floor. "I'm sorry. Can you repeat that? I guess I couldn't hear properly over the sound of me punching you in the head."

"I said... leave us... alone. Okay?" Paul tries hard not to hyperventilate.

Pitty shifts his weight from one foot to the other, his face smug as a hoard of locusts. "Or what?" he says.

Paul doesn't respond.

"Leave. You. Alone. Or. What?" Pitty continues, poking his finger into Paul's chest with each word. Paul braces for the inevitable, something more substantial than a finger-jab. But all of a sudden Fanta steps between them, throwing everybody off guard.

"Or this," she says to Pitty, her voice surprisingly calm. "My father, who's a lawyer, brings you up on charges. Voyeurism, public mischief, uttering threats, and maybe one or two other things I haven't thought of yet. I have a very good imagination. And I'm just getting started."

Paul can see the hamster wheel turning in Pitty's head. He's been to the cop shop a couple times already this year, once for minor-league theft and then that night he set the garbage bin on fire beside the high school. After the last incident his counsellor told him, "The general rule is three strikes and you're out, Mr. Pittman. That means you're one fuck-up away from having to exit the diamond. Understand?"

Whether Fanta knows about that or not doesn't matter; Paul's pretty sure her father isn't a lawyer.

"No need to get *legal*," Pitty says finally. He waves his hand in the air and steps backwards. "We're just leaving anyway. Go ahead and finish your game of hide-and-go-fuck-yourselves or whatever you two shit-birds were doing."

He stumbles out of the gazebo, fingering them over his shoulder as he goes. The sidekick-guy does the same and they both disappear along the path towards town.

Before Paul can say anything or even start breathing again, Fanta kisses him for what seems like forever. It's almost too much to process.

After they stop, she outlines his lips, slowly, with the tip of her finger. "And now that all the weirdness is over and the

night, still young," she says, "what do you say to a little moonlight dip?"

Eric follows Marilyn as she hands out the tarts and cream.
He offers water to everyone but doesn't go anywhere near the
new bottles of wine. He'll let Kip fumble that grenade. He
knows it isn't enough to have declined another glass himself
but it can't have hurt. He did it loudly too, so Marilyn wouldn't
miss it. And now whenever he walks by, he makes sure to touch
her arm or her lower back. So she knows he's still there.

"Perfect tarts, Marilyn," Lisa says. "Recipe please."

"Thank you. But they're pretty easy."

"Don't be humble, honey. You're a divine chef," Eric says.
Then he adds, "I'm a lucky, lucky man."

Marilyn ignores him. She asks, "Would anyone like coffee
before we continue?"

"I'm good with wine," Kip says, refilling everyone's glasses.

Marilyn sighs. She collects the dirty dishes and goes back
into the kitchen.

"I'll help," Eric calls out.

He finds her in front of the sink, rinsing plates, and walks
up behind her. "Don't," she tells him before he even gets close.

Eric stands there. He's not really sure what to do so he does
nothing. After a minute or so, Marilyn finally says, "Maybe it's
us who're broken. Not Paul."

Eric closes his eyes. More than anything he wants to put
his arms around his wife, make everything better. But the question is does he want to do it for her or for him?

"I've been an asshole, and I want to be part of the team
again," he says. "You and me."

Marilyn turns around but Eric doesn't wait to hear what she
might have to say. In fact, he's a little bit afraid of it. Back in the
living room, he collects the half-full bottles of wine and puts
them off to the side while his wife watches from the doorway.

"Break's over," he says to the bewildered faces. "It's my turn
to speak again. For real this time."

PAUL FOLLOWS FANTA into the lake. He's naked, but doesn't shield himself as he enters the water. And his blood is pumping so fast he hardly feels the coldness, even when it reaches his groin. Fanta, ahead of him, dives in and disappears. She pops up a few seconds later and starts swimming backwards. "Come on," she says. In the darkness, Paul sees the moon shining off her skin.

"Be right there," he answers, waving his hand like he's signalling a helicopter. The water's all the way to his chest now, touching his chin, and he launches his feet as he gets past the point where he can feel bottom.

Earlier, during the incident at the gazebo, he imagined his adrenaline firing at a hundred percent. But now that he's here—alone with Fanta in the lake, both of them naked—it's more than double that. She's halfway to the dock already and Paul watches her arms rise and plunge, hardly making a ripple. She's a terrific swimmer, no question about it. But he's not. In fact, he's already getting tired.

He changes kicks for a while, but when he does he starts to sink and some of the lake gets into his mouth. He struggles to get going again, to catch up before Fanta leaves him behind, before she disappears completely. And suddenly his heart... his heart doesn't feel so good.

He remembers when he was young and his parents wanted him to take swimming lessons. He got that same tightness in his chest back then. A balled up mass of staples in his core, pumping into his veins and pinching through every inch of his body. He's never told anyone about it before because as long as he avoided anything strenuous, he felt okay. Right now though, everything inside him feels like it's being squeezed, then ripped apart. Squeezed. Ripped apart. Squeezed.

His head goes under and his lungs expand, trying to suck in air. He comes up coughing and spitting out water. He can't hear any of it though, his sputtering, his splashing. All he hears is the rush of blood in his ears and the whirr of the aerator off to the side. He flips onto his back and tries to swim that way but the pain in his chest gets worse. He turns over again and clutches his arms to his body. And starts to sink.

Just before he goes under he sees Fanta pulling herself up on the dock. The long curve of her back, her beautiful skin. She turns and sees him struggling in the water, and she jumps back in. But she's so far away. So incredibly far away...

When he's fully submerged, he squeezes his legs to his chest to stop the pain and thinks about how his parents are going to hate him for this. Oh God. Oh God. They're going to hate him forever.

MARILYN FEELS LIKE CRYING by the time Eric's finished. She hugs him, squeezing tightly despite the fact it's not in keeping with her role as moderator. She doesn't care about that though. Or about anything. For the first time in years, she actually feels like things are going to be okay.

The others, led by Kip, begin to applaud at their embrace and the speech her husband just gave. And that *does* make her cry.

Eric pulls back. He smiles and whispers in her ear. She doesn't quite hear it though; she's distracted by a commotion outside the window. Lights flashing. A police car pulling up. And another one.

There's someone familiar, Marilyn notices, sitting in the back of the nearest car. A girl she's seen before from school a few times, one of Paul's friends. She looks pretty upset, shaking her head and running her hands through her hair. The lights, flashing all over her face.

But is she alone in the car, this girl? Hard to tell with the windows fogged up and Marilyn's eyes still wet with tears. She looks again, squinting hard. And yes, someone else. Right there in the seat beside her. She's absolutely, positively sure of it.

Maybe.

"So what have our teenagers done now?" she says to the group, trying to quell the energy so she doesn't lose this perfect moment. The clapping behind them abruptly stops.

LOST VALLEY

GRANDDAD CALLS IT *BEDLAM-WEATHER*, the sort of day
that makes people act like lunatics. But me, I love
the heat. I'd live half-naked in the blazing sun if
I was allowed to take my shirt off. Of course if I took mine
off, Riley would too and Mom's made that a *don't-even-think-
about-it* item. Riley's sitting in the sandbox by the fence: long
sleeves, pants, goofy hat with the Arabian neck flap. He's got
the banged-up Tonkas, using them to fill his shoes with dirt.
Brilliant kid, my brother. Sometimes I wonder just what goes
on inside his big, dopey head.

This morning, the guy on the radio said the whole summer
would be hot but Mom says the weatherman can't predict a
fart from his own arse so we shouldn't put too much stock in it.
The first day off school's a scorcher, though, no question there.
I just finished Grade Five and Riley, Kindergarten.

I feel a breeze blowing down from the Martinez place, warm
and stale, the type of wind that carries angry bees. Everything
around us seems clear, though. Nothing weird in the yard except
the fact Riley has no shoes anymore. He's completely buried
them now, starting on his socks. I can't blame him either. Shoes,
socks, in this heat. I almost feel sorry for the little stink.

I put my comic down and stretch out in the hammock. The tarp on the woodpile beside me rises and falls with the wind; the wood beneath, un-chopped since last summer. This morning Mom got up from the breakfast table and pointed at it. She threw her coffee cup out the window and said, "Maybe this mug will chop that wood. No? Useless then, hey Gary. I guess that mug is useless."

"Who wants to think about firewood in this heat?" Dad said, a clump of hair hanging down in an arc over his forehead. He smiled, but Mom wasn't having it.

"Lots of bachelor suites in town *without* fireplaces," she said. "Or you could always go live with your idiot father. He doesn't have a fireplace either. Oh, Christ—Terry, Riley, go get ready. Your grandfather will be here soon."

Riley glommed onto me after that like the grade A sissy he is. Every time Mom yells, he sticks closer than a blackberry stain. Once he even climbed in the top bunk with me while I slept. I woke in the middle of the night to find half my pyjama top clenched between his fists. Snuggling my shirt like a friggin' teddy bear.

Mom's cup still sits along the fence line; she has a pretty good arm.

We live on a big chunk of land in a woody development called *The Acreage,* twenty minutes from town. Dad doesn't care one way or the other, but Mom likes having a big lot. She's at the kitchen window right now, hands digging deep into the sink. There's a tea towel around her neck which makes her look like a six o'clock TV boxer. A hot day like this gives her a boxer's temperament too, so I'm glad to be outside.

Dad comes through the back door with his briefcase and a box of books to sell. He stands there sweating in his brown suit like he's dressed for church. I picture him dragging his samples and order forms from house to house. People shaking their heads, holding their arms up, showing him the palms of their hands. Mom says he should be more aggressive, jam a foot right in the door. I look down at Dad's shoes—they're gleaming in the sunshine.

"You boys heed your mother, okay? She's... I'll be back later." He takes a step towards Riley, then turns and picks up Mom's coffee mug. He twists it in the sun for a long time, puts it in the box and walks around the house. I hear the car exhaust fluttering and spitting as he creeps away down the drive.

I roll up my sleeves and return to my comic, *Turok: Son of Stone*, my favourite series. Two men trapped in Lost Valley, trying to find their way home. In this issue, Andar is sick. He drank from the wrong pool and Turok's searching for the medicine herb to cure him. I don't know if Andar's gonna make it, he looks pretty bad, and I don't have the next comic where the story continues on. But maybe later I'll get lucky. Granddad's barber in town sells magazines in the back and each month he gives away old stock. Today, Granddad's taking me with him while Cadwell Drace cuts his hair. Riley's coming too. Mom's orders.

I hear Granddad's car zip up the drive and I jump from the hammock to meet him. Riley brushes himself off and follows. "Wait up," he yells. I run faster.

Granddad drives a banana-coloured '69 El Camino with an engine you can hear a mile away. A plume of dust follows the car, circling it like a sneeze when he comes to a stop in front of the house. He gets out and walks towards me, hunched over with his hand on his lower back, dragging one leg behind him. I know better—it's Granddad's rope-a-dope. As soon as he gets close, he fake punches me in the side and flips me over his shoulder, ducking under the doorframe into the house.

"Hey there, Rosemarie," Granddad says. My mother comes around the corner, the tea towel still wrapped around her neck.

"Oh, Ernie. My God, put the child down. Your back... his head..."

Granddad fakes a muscle spasm and then sets me on the rug in front of the door. Riley trots in and Granddad spider-claws his neck until he squeaks out a laugh.

"Where's Gary?" Granddad asks.

"You know him, always gone." Mom throws her arms in the air, pinches her lips together so hard they almost disappear. "It'd be different if he had a good job, you know, but ah!"

Riley stops giggling and inches towards me.

Mom shakes her head, gearing up. I know what's coming next and my grandfather must too because he scoops me up again, grabs Riley and says, "We're going to town."

AT THE BARBERSHOP, Mr. Drace lets me sit in the chair when he's finished with Granddad. I tell him Mom usually does the haircuts in our family, and he grins and promises there'll be no charge at all. Riley's sitting cross-legged on the rug, sucking on a yellow Popsicle. He's too chicken to want a seat in the big chair and that's fine by me.

"Well, Terrence. What would you like? Longer in the back, thicker up top?" Mr. Drace says. He rubs my flat, red hair with his hand. Mom once called it a field of wilted poppies.

"I don't know," I shrug as he snaps the black cloak over me and ties it behind my neck. It's hot underneath the cape but it covers my whole body and I like that. Mr. Drace holds his scissors by the blades, taps the handle against his chin as he examines my hair. I smell cigarette smoke on his clothes and a spicy almond cologne.

"So what about you? You got a girl in your life?" he asks, a continuation of the conversation he and Granddad had earlier. In the mirror beside me, Granddad waxes his moustache with his fingers. His hair, Brylcreem-ed back in perfect, grey lines that curve around his head like the grooves on a record.

"No way," I say.

Mr. Drace laughs. A loud, smack of a noise.

"You hear that, Ernie? Another happy bachelor." He starts to snip and a little orange tuft falls on my nose. He swishes it away with the end of his comb.

"Yup," Granddad answers. But his forehead is wrinkled like he's thinking about something else altogether.

Mr. Drace finishes the trim and rubs a drop of gel through my hair. "Yeah. That's it," he says. "You look like a bullfighter now, eh Terrence?" I look over to see what everyone thinks but Riley's fiddling with a shoelace on Granddad's wingtips, distracting him. I jump down from the chair and Mr. Drace gives me what I've been waiting for this whole time—a thick roll of comics wrapped with an elastic band. "See what you make of these," he says. I stuff the roll in my back pocket and flip my shirt overtop.

Mr. Drace shakes my grandfather's hand. "You going over to Gally's?" he asks.

Granddad nods.

Then Mr. Drace gives him another stack of magazines. On the cover of the top one I see a car painted black with orange and red flames. There's a woman on the hood wearing short-shorts but Granddad folds the book before I can really make it out.

"See you later, Drace," Granddad says. At the door I hear him whisper something else before we leave. Something that sounds a lot like, "Wish us luck."

GRANDDAD THROWS HALF THE MAGAZINES under his seat and the rest into a cardboard box in the back of the car. "Wait here," he says, heading across the street. Beside me, Riley is quiet for once, his face red as an Indian paintbrush.

"Take off your hat," I say.

"Mom told me..."

"Mom's not here, goof. Take it off." I grab his stupid flap-hat and pull it away. His hair is drenched.

I'm dying to check out the stories rolled up in my pocket, to see if Turok's in there saving Andar, but by the time I finish wiping Riley's dumb head and calming him down, Granddad's back with some bags from the liquor store and grocery. He throws them in the back with the magazines and pulls a couple suckers from his pocket. I let Riley have the red one 'cause for sure he'd cry if I didn't.

"We have to make a stop before I bring you boys home. It's on the way," Granddad says, firing up the car. He doesn't say anything else but I know exactly where we're going—Galeno Martinez's house, the neighbour beside us in the acreage. Granddad picks up supplies for Galeno all the time but he usually drops us off before delivering them. It's another of Mom's rules and she reminds us about it every chance she gets.

Mom says Galeno's a kook—sharp as an egg, she calls him— and even Dad says to steer clear of his place. At school, Jimmy

Po from Grade Six told me Galeno has weird animals all over his yard like some kind of Hallowe'en petting zoo. Chickens and pigs right inside the house. I don't know about that, but the real reason Mom and Dad want us to stay away is something else altogether. Galeno keeps honeybees. Tons of them.

Last year at a Canada Day picnic, Riley stepped on a bee in a patch of clover. His foot got all fat and spotty from the sting so now I have to carry Sudafed in my pocket wherever we go. If Riley ever got bit, Mom would blame me, like I have control over the world of insects. Like it's my job to watch out for the dufus. I don't know what the fuss is about anyway. It was just a case of the itches.

We pull into Galeno's yard and Riley scrunches his face into a world-class pout. "Stay here," Granddad tells us, heading for the door under the covered porch.

The steps are steep and the wood looks old, the colour of elephant skin. Some ragged chickens peck at the ground behind a fence to the left. They snap at each other's feet, hopping around a blown-out truck tire while Galeno's mongrel dog barks at them from the end of a chain. Raspberry bushes line one wall of the house, so wild and out of control they're crawling right up on the roof. And off to the side, not more than a pee-stream away, sit a couple of big, pine beehives.

The hives are homemade jobs, long as coffins except skinny at the base. There's a piece of tin roofing over the top and a bunch of holes drilled in the side for the bees to go in and out. I notice Galeno has a hat with a mesh face, some thick gloves, and two spray bottles hanging on hooks by the front door. I roll down the window to catch a whiff of honeycomb, and I hear the insects buzzing, loud and steady as a power line. I can almost feel the wing vibrations from here, from the cab of the El Camino.

Riley starts to fidget.

I've got half a mind to feed the little pecker to those hungry bees. Instead, I say, "Look at Granddad? Don't see him freakin' do ya?"

Granddad puts the box down and bangs on the screen door.

"I'm telling Mom," Riley says. He wipes his nose with his sleeve.

"No you're not."

I pull out the roll of comics. Riley stops whining and peeks over my shoulder. I let him see just enough to keep him quiet. There are a couple of *Unknown Soldiers* in the pile, an *Archie,* and two consecutive issues of *Turok.* Straight off in the first one there's a picture of Andar. He's getting sicker.

Granddad yells at us from the porch. "Hey, you two. Come inside for a second," he says. "I've got a job for you."

WE WIPE OUR SHOES on a dirty, oval rug at the entrance. Then Riley clutches Granddad's leg and we follow him down the hallway. Photographs line the walls on both sides of us: a sunrise over a lake, a group of women dressed in old-style skirts and bonnets, a man in a chequered shirt kneeling beside a dead deer, its chin propped up on the man's boot. There's another picture in a wooden frame with this same man. In this one, he's wearing a suit, standing beside a woman in a flowery dress. She's quite big but pretty as a movie star, and the man, all stiff and nervous like he's got arrows taped to his arms. Galeno.

We go around a corner into the kitchen and Galeno's there, sitting on a green chair at a matching table. His sleeves are worn and there's a greasy sheen to his hair and forehead. Two stubby bottles of beer and a loaf of white bread sit in front of him. And although he's a lot younger than my grandfather, to look at him, here in his kitchen, you'd swear he and Granddad were the same age. When he notices us, he teeters like he's about to tip over.

"Want a little dough, huh?" He squints at Riley and me.

Granddad sits down on the only other chair in the kitchen and takes a swig of beer. "Sure they do. Look at 'em, Gally. Hard workers, the both." He winks and I feel a little better about whatever it is Galeno wants. "They'll be careful, too. Don't worry. Gentle as two butterflies."

"Well, go on then. Get to it." Galeno points his finger at a closed door in the hall behind us.

"All right. I'll get them started." Granddad gets up, grabs

a package of garbage bags from the groceries, and takes us into the room across the hall.

The room isn't filled with pigs and chickens like I'd expected. It's just a regular room, hot, stale, and dusty. There's a bed covered with a beige afghan, two pillows with sunflowers on the cases, a chest of drawers, nightstand, a tall mirror hanging in the corner. And the bedroom curtains—deep orange and thick as a tarp—are faded in the middle in a perfect window-sized square.

"Sit," Granddad says.

I move to the bed and Riley hops up beside me.

"Galeno wants to get rid of some stuff. Empty everything into these garbage bags, but do it carefully." He sits down with us, deep into the mattress, and waits for the springs to stop squeaking. "Gally's wife died. A time ago, but still. This stuff belonged to her and he wants it out now."

Riley bounces his bum on the bed; I swat his arm.

"It's all going to the Salvation Army," Granddad continues, examining his hands slowly as if he was holding a small bird. Something made of glass.

"How?" I ask.

"Hmm?"

"How did she die?"

"Childbirth. The baby too," he says. "So many years, they tried." He shakes his head and leaves us to the job.

THE DRAWERS OF THE NIGHTSTAND are small so I get Riley started there while I open the heavy orange curtains. The window's wedged closed with a long piece of wood that I have to dig out with my fingernail. There isn't a screen in the room, but I open the window all the way anyhow.

Riley freezes in front of the night table, the whining-machine inside him firing up again. "Get going," I say, grabbing a bunch of shirts from the dresser and shoving them into a bag. Instead of listening, Riley skulks over to the same drawer as me, his face scrunched up like he just ate a grapefruit.

"Be useful at least and hold the bag, bum-ass," I tell him.

He grabs it and his arms drop.

"Hold it *up*."

I toss a couple of sweatshirts and some socks into the bag, trying to ignore Riley's annoying face. I've seen it a million times, the fat-lip thing he does when he knows it's stupid to cry. I take one of the shirts, a light blue blouse with frills, and hold it to my chest, twisting like a swimsuit model to make Riley forget about being a suck-hole. He grins and I throw the shirt into the bag with the others.

At the bottom of the drawer I find a photograph, the same woman from the picture in the hallway. She's sitting in a field of wildflowers staring at a daisy, her white dress spread around her like spilled milk.

When Riley's not looking, I put it in my back pocket.

The next drawer holds Galeno's wife's underwear. I pull out a bra so big it looks like two catcher's mitts sewn together. Riley gets the giggles and even I start to laugh. When I hold it over my head, Riley goes hysterical.

"What's that?" he says after he calms down, pointing at the bra.

I take a closer look and see a flap opening in the middle of each cup like two trap doors fastened by silver buttons. There's a price tag as well, hanging from a plastic wire. I throw it in the bag and clear the rest of the drawer in one big scoop.

Riley's still laughing.

"Shut up," I say.

"What for?"

"Shut up," I say again, and I grab another bag from the pile.

GALENO AND GRANDDAD are still at the table when we're finished, a few more empty bottles lined up in front of them.

"We're done," I say, and Riley comes up behind me, clinging to my shirt like a pondweed. I shake him off and move beside Granddad.

"Good boys, you two. You're good boys, you hear?" Galeno says. He nods at us like we just put out a fire on his arm. Like we did something big. "Have a drink? All right? Something, I think."

Galeno gets up. He stands for a second getting his balance, then moves over to the fridge. There are finger smudges all over the front and when he opens it, the light doesn't go on. "Coke-y-cola, okay?" Galeno pulls a bottle out and smiles; his teeth are the same faded yellow as the armpits of his shirt. He takes two glasses from the cupboard and blows into them before pouring. Then he grabs some bread from the bag on the table, drizzles honey on a couple pieces and smoothes it out with the back of a spoon. One for me and one for Riley.

"From the bees," he says, tilting his neck towards the window. "They work hard all the time. Taking care of the queen, building the combs. Like a giant family. One bee, alone, that's worse than nothing. But together..." He lifts the honey jar to show us. A milky amber colour, like Mom's strong tea with cream.

I take a bite of my bread. It's a little hard but the honey is amazing and I gobble the whole thing in no time. Riley savours his though, licking the slice until it's bare before eating it. For the first time all day, he's being normal.

"You guys work hard too," Galeno goes on. "Brothers, all the time. You don't know how it is though. Don't wanna ever know, you see?"

I don't see, but I nod anyway and sip my Coke.

"Nothing lasts, eh Ernie? Nothing ever lasts." Galeno puts his head down.

Granddad motions for us to finish our drinks. "Gotta take these kids home. You'll be okay now, Gally."

"Okay. I'm okay." Galeno looks like he's about to get up but he stops. Like he's too weak, like he's sick. "The box by the door. You take that for the boys, all right? You take that box," he says.

The three of us carry the bags from the bedroom and pile them into the back of the El Camino, Galeno's dog barking the whole time we're in the yard. Then Granddad returns for Galeno's box. He shows us before loading it in the back—twelve full mason jars. Galeno's paying us with honey. Granddad wipes his hands on his pants, gets in the car, and we slowly pull away from the house.

THE DRIVE FROM GALENO'S takes less than a minute but it feels much longer. When we get close, Granddad reaches into his pocket and gives us each two dollars for our work. Riley's more excited about the honey than the cash though, keeping his eyes on the jars like they're going to fly away in the breeze. We never have honey around our place.

"Put your hat back on," I tell my brother as we park in the driveway.

Granddad takes the honey from the back and hands it to me. "I've got to take these other things to the Sally Ann before she closes," he says, messing my hair and squeezing Riley's neck before getting back in the car. "It's my fault we're late, tell your mom. Don't let her take it out on your dad." Granddad's talking to me but Riley nods too.

Just as he pulls away, Mom comes outside. "Where were you guys?" she says. "Bad enough your father... What the hell happened to your hair?"

"Well, Mr. Drace…"

"And what's that?" Mom points at the honey with a wooden spoon stained pink from spaghetti sauce, her forehead dripping with sweat. Riley creeps behind me, quiet as a spider. Abandoning me, full face in the line of fire.

"Honey," I say. Mom gives me one of her volcano-looks.

"I see that. Where did you get it?" She presses forward.

"Granddad took us," I say. "So we went and helped and got some honey."

"And some money," Riley pipes in. He sticks out his arm and waves the bills in the air like two little flags.

"We worked for it," I say. "Even Riley did, hey Riley?" His chin bounces off my back as he nods.

"Galeno Martinez?" Mom guesses. "With Riley? Are you crazy?"

"We were inside the whole time. Granddad said it was okay."

Mom advances. She lifts the spoon and brings it down across the knuckles of my left hand. The spoon and the box both fall to the ground with a couple of muted pops. And the honey, watery from the heat, starts to run out on the soil.

"Your grandfather is an idiot. Just like his son. And you two should know better."

Mom goes inside. Riley crouches down and pokes at the spilled honey while I rub my knuckles. I'm about to tell him most of the jars didn't bust so he won't start bawling but Mom comes right back out.

"Pick up that box," she tells me. "Let's go."

I do what she says and we follow her, the whole left side of my shirt curled up in Riley's fingers. He isn't crying though. No grapefruit-face this time either. That's something at least.

My arms start to ache from carrying the box. And the dripping honey leaves sticky lines all the way down to my knees. I keep thinking if Dad was here then Mom would have someone else to yell at and everything would be normal again. But we just keep walking.

When we get to the edge of Galeno's driveway, about a hundred feet from the house, Mom grabs the box from me. "Stay here," she says. Riley glances at the two long beehives. Galeno comes to the door and his dog starts barking from his chain. I strain to listen.

"What, exactly, the fuck is wrong with you?" Mom says.

Galeno shakes his head. It seems like he really doesn't know what my mother is yelling about. He just stands there raising his arms, putting them back down. Scratching the back of his neck.

"Don't shake your head at me," Mom yells. She shoves the box of honey at him, knocking him on his butt; jars and broken glass fly all over the porch. One jar rolls slowly down the stairs, clunking each step like a boot, leaving a thick, sticky trail behind it. Galeno sits motionless while Mom screams, swarming around him in a frenzy that—even for her—seems excessive. Then something tickles my hand, I can't ignore it. A bee walking around on my knuckles, going after the honey. I swat it away and back up a couple of steps.

That's when I notice Riley isn't behind me anymore.

His shirt is on the ground, his hat, his shoes. But no Riley. I look up and see him walking towards the side of the house, over to the hives. He slips off his pants as he walks, barely slowing down. There's something long and thin in his right hand— Mom's wooden spoon—swaying beside him.

Mom's oblivious. Still screaming at Galeno, hunched over him like a grizzly bear. Riley's past the far end of the house now; I start to run. "Hey. Hey," I scream, but Galeno's barking dog drowns it out. Riley's already at the first hive, completely naked. He holds his arm up.

"*Hey!*" I yell again just as he brings the spoon down, hard, on the hive's tin roof.

Mom stops yelling and turns. "Oh my God," she says.

My brother beats the hive over and over like he's cleaning a rug; the wood around the holes becomes dark with bees. They fly around him as he moves on to the second hive, whacking the top of it as well. They're crawling on the tin and the spoon. The air, thick with them. And there's nothing I can do to stop it.

Then I feel someone's arm across my chest. Galeno.

"Wait," he says, running towards the hives. He has a plastic spray bottle in each hand, the ones from the wall. He starts spraying a fine mist over the bees and they focus on him. Landing on the honey stuck to his jeans, crawling all over the bottles. Riley steps backwards to get out of the way but he seems lost—squinting at the sun, the air, the yard—like he just stepped out of a cave.

"Get the boy," Galeno says to me, still squirting the bees with the mist. "Slowly."

I grab the end of Riley's spoon and walk backwards, dragging him with me. Bees buzz in the tangle of his hair and a couple have landed on his chest and crotch. I feel one crawling around the outside of my ear. We keep moving until we get to the porch and then Mom brushes Riley off. Soon as she has him, I swat my ear, my shoulder, a few other places.

"What were you doing? Oh, Riley," Mom says inside Galeno's house, her voice fluttery, hardly sounding like her at all. She searches Riley's body for stings. Checks his armpits, his fingers, the back of his neck.

The screen door bangs as Galeno finally joins us, welts swelling up on his hands and face. "Okay, now?" he says. "The mom and the boy. All okay now?"

DAD'S HOME FROM WORK by the time we get back. He examines Riley from head to toe—not a single sting, nothing. He's lucky, my brother. Crazy as hell, but lucky. I go outside when Dad finishes his inspection. The sun is almost down but it's still hot and the air smells coppery, like heat-lightning or a coming rain. No clouds anywhere in the sky though, and I don't really know what that means.

Galeno must've told Granddad about the incident. We're only home for an hour when he shows up in the El Camino, bouncing and skidding in the dirt as he slams on the brakes.

"Is he all right?" Granddad asks.

I nod from my seat on the stairs. He nods back, wipes the sweat from his chin, and goes through the door.

I stay outside and read in the fading light, flipping quickly through both issues of Turok. Nothing's changed by the end of the comics and I wonder if those two will ever find their way out of the valley. It's close to bedtime and everything is quiet, so I go in.

Granddad and Dad sit at the kitchen table, two tall glasses between them. Dad has my grandfather's hand between his. When he sees me, he jerks his head, waving me on.

I walk past Mom and Dad's room. A couple brown suits lie in a pile on the bed and there's an open suitcase by the closet. I hear Mom in the bathroom but I don't want to talk to her so I head straight to Riley's and my bedroom.

Riley's in his bunk already. His eyes are closed and his cheeks, shiny and damp. I pull the photograph I took from Galeno's drawer out of my pocket and stuff it between the pages of a comic. After a few days when things cool down, I'll bring it back over to Galeno. I'm sure he'll want to keep it.

I shove the comic under my pillow and lean down to check Riley again. As soon as I look, he re-shuts his eyes and doesn't move. Hardly even breathes, the little faker. It's going to be a long night. Maybe a string of them. So I put on my PJs, the ones with the softest, baggiest shirt, and climb into Riley's bed with him. I'll only stay here for a little while though, just because he's the way he is, just because he's my brother. Just until he closes his eyes for real and actually falls asleep.

INTO THE SUNSET

"I THINK WE'RE OUT OF THE WOODS," Misty tells me. It's funny because we are, for the first time, actually in the woods. Also because she hasn't noticed the blood.

"Sure thing," I say. "Apple pie order, first class."

She crawls towards me, small twigs cracking under her knees and hands. I'm lying in the moss against a rock, holding the bison head because I don't have a choice. I know the wound is bad even though nothing like this has ever happened to me before. The coldness gives it away.

"Colin. Oh my God."

She puts her hand on my chest. I don't think she'll faint though; she's seen bad things before. And when I think about *that* I'm embarrassed to have ever complained about anything in my entire life.

I picture the dog at home in that bedroom. Lying on the mat below the aging crib. When my parents find him they'll know something's wrong and they'll worry like they always do. Only this time—for the first time and on this of all nights—they'll be right.

"Stay awake!" Misty tells me. I didn't know I was sleeping.

She lies beside me and I feel her tug the blood-soaked glove

149

off my hand. Then she leans close, next to my ear, and I wonder if she'll cover my eyes with coins, chase away wolves, pull out a flask. Then I don't wonder anymore. But her fingers are warm at least, and her cheek, right next to mine.

"I'm cold," I tell her.

She brushes the hair, gently, from my forehead. Kisses my eyebrow and says, "You don't have to worry about being alone, Colin. We're weird partners, remember? And *partners* means forever."

MISTY CLIMBS ON THE BISON and I give it a push before hopping up. We start rolling, and behind us Misty's mom and Pete crest the hill. Pete doubles over, sucking in air while Misty's mom gives us the finger. They look ridiculous, cartoon villains in a cloud of getaway dust. He lights a cigarette and shrugs us off, yells something we can't hear. They head in the other direction.

"They've gone," I tell her over the rumble of the wheels.

She squeezes my fingers. "This buffalo is fast!"

"Actually it's a... yes. It's a fast buffalo."

It's true, we *are* picking up speed. The hill in front of us goes on forever and I just greased the axles last week, routine maintenance. And then there's the weight of the thing, the metal plate alone is almost a hundred pounds. "Hang on," I say. The wind blowing her hair all around me.

It's beautiful I think, the two of us riding off. Somewhere between being completely smothered and totally unwanted. There's a special word for it I'm sure, but I don't want to think about it right now. I just want to enjoy this one small moment.

I remember something else: the road we're on, it ends. Very soon in a cul-de-sac with only a mossy hiking trail at the base. It's too dark to see but I know it's coming.

"Hang on," I say again. And I grab her waist with my free arm as we approach the pavement's end.

At first we keep going. Then the wheels dig in and the bison slides sideways. I'd been pulling back on the reins for most of the hill—pretty stupid. But now I wrap both arms around Misty and twist my body to shield her as the bison goes down. We're launched into the air and I hope she knows I'm being noble here. It's not noble, I know, to *want* to be noble. But still, it's all I've got.

We hit the ground and roll for a while, my arms held tight around her. When we stop I see the bison sliding towards us, the full weight of it, the spinning wheels.

The horns.

I shove Misty out of the way and feel them pressing in. Doesn't hurt, but I'm pinned against the boulder and can't move. I hold my breath and listen, just to know that Misty's okay. That she's still there behind me. That she hasn't, somehow in the darkness of the night, disappeared.

THE BISON ROLLS QUICKLY and we gain some ground, mostly because Misty's mom is plastered and Pete the salesman is pretty fat. At the end of Agate Lane though, just before the road to the water tower, the asphalt turns gravelly and the wheels get stuck on all the pebbles. I check Misty's face while I manoeuver and her eyes remind me of the women in old westerns, the ones who take it and take it and take it until finally…

"What now, fuckers," Pete yells. He's wheezy and damp and I imagine somehow even the inside of his mouth is sweating.

"I'll tell you *what*," Misty's mom adds. She doesn't, however, say anything else.

The grade gets steeper as I guide us through the minefield of rocks and I hear Pete and Misty's mom closing the gap. We can't outrun them—uphill, pushing the bison—I know. Pete knows it too and he starts whooping while Misty's mom remains silent. I can't decide which is worse.

Misty jumps off the bison. I stop pushing and engage the brakes while she turns to face our pursuers.

"I knew I raised a sensible girl," her mother says. "Even if sense comes late and now my night is ruined." She glances at the stars, like there's some burden there we can't possibly see. And she flicks her lighter. On. Off. On. Off. On.

Misty starts towards her.

"Wait. Don't leave me," I say. I don't know why, it just comes out.

She stops a few feet from her mother and I follow to stand beside her. We touch hands and it's one of those moments. The moonlight. Then she bends down and picks up the biggest, most jagged rock she can find.

I pull the oilskin glove from my pocket and slip it on.

"Sweetie? It's only me," her mother says, turning her head to the side like a cat you've been warned about.

"Oh yes, Mother," Misty answers. "We know exactly who you are."

She cocks her arm and I think about those scars again. I want to touch them right here in front of her mother so she knows I'm on to her.

But this is Misty's moment, not mine.

I try to imagine what Misty's thinking during this standoff. All I know is her mother deserves it, every single word of what isn't being said right now, here between them. Finally, Misty touches my elbow. "Keep pushing," she says.

I walk backwards until I reach the bison. And I disengage the brakes.

Misty's mom starts yelling, something about family, but Misty's not buying it. She's not throwing the rock either, just giving me the time I need. When I'm just about at the top, she joins me and starts pushing too.

The other side of the hill heads off into the valley. It's longer and much, much steeper than the side we've just climbed.

"Shall we?" I say, motioning to the bison with my newly-gloved hand.

The look on her face tells it all.

"OH GOD. IT'S MY MOTHER," Misty says. Instinctively, we duck behind the bison.

The woman we're looking at is smoking three cigarettes at once and laughing about how funny that is. She's skinny, dressed in jean-everything, standing outside Snackity Jack's, a stupidly-named convenience store that sells magazines, slushies, and nachos from a machine.

"I don't know the guy she's with though." Misty pauses,

shielding her eyes from the streetlights beyond. "He's new to the rotation."

"It's Pete Smithers, the car salesman," I tell her. I know she doesn't really care about the name, I just don't know what else to say.

Pete sold my parents a Volvo, years ago. At first they weren't sure about the deal but then he went on about his bad case of shingles and the SPCA cat he rescued with liver problems. The clincher—which showed he'd done his homework on my folks—was when he pulled out the crash-safety record on the model he was flogging. Specifically, backseat-passenger protection. "To keep our children safe," he said. The contract almost signed itself.

"I'm supposed to be at home right now," Misty goes on, running her fingers along the skin of her arm.

"Me too."

"Yeah, but *your* mother never said, *Abortion was my first choice, honey, but I flipped a coin.* Did she?"

"Everything will be okay," I tell her. Then I picture my parents in the living room watching the clock like a couple of undertakers and I almost add, *Everyone's folks are messed up, Misty, you don't get to pick who you ride the river with.*

But I don't.

Suddenly, Pete turns and squints at us with his dirty salesman's eyes. He lifts a finger and points in our direction. "Hey, isn't that a buffalo over there?" he says. "And also... *your daughter?*"

Misty's mom stiffens. She turns and her expression makes me think of insects. She drops the cigarettes, one by one, and snuffs them out with the heel of her shoe.

I think about what I saw earlier, what I felt on Misty's skin, and I know we have but one option.

"Get on," I tell Misty who's literally shaking at this point and I have to use my hands as a makeshift stirrup. Once she's in position, I run behind the bison, dig in with my replica boots, and push.

MISTY DOES RECONNAISSANCE; everything's deserted so she gives me the all-clear. She does a little dance on the sidewalk, stomping her feet like she's testing the planks on a trestle. I realize I don't know much about her although we've been class-mates for years. We even sat beside each other this semester and still, never talked. Nobody's fault of course; she's intensely shy, I'm intensely shy. Maybe that's why we're good seatmates, why we're a good fit now. I can't explain it other than that and really, does it matter?

Together, we wheel the bison out the door, down the ramp, past the welcome sign with the bad carving of Daniel Boone. We take the alley between the liquor store and post office, lis-tening to the buzz of the streetlamps as we go. It's a strange kind of music: the stillness of the air, the echo of our feet. The rhythm of three wandering ghosts. That's what I'm thinking as we—Misty and I and the stuffed bison—stroll down the streets of our town.

We end up in the parking lot for *High Valley Foods* and I tie the Bison's "reins" around a sign pole, resisting the urge to shoot a finger-thumb gun, fake-tip an invisible hat. Sometimes you can take a thing too far.

Misty's face lights up and she raises an eyebrow. "Can I… go for a ride?" she says. The shine of her eyes in the night.

Nobody's actually been on the bison before, not even me. It's part of my job, making sure people stay off the displays, so even though it's built like a mountain I should tell her, *it isn't safe*. It's what my parents would say, absolutely. What they've been saying to me my entire life.

"You know what?" I tell her instead, my heart pounding. "I think that's the best idea I've ever heard." And I help her climb aboard.

I wheel her around the parking lot, back and forth in a long sweeping grid like we're part of a search party. After a while, I speed up and even stand on the wheel-plate, holding the Bison's flank for support. I try to stay cool even though being cool isn't my strong point. When it comes to rebellion, any kind of rebellion, I'm the biggest rookie in town.

There's a depression in the middle of the parking lot and the momentum there gives us butterflies. Soon, we're scream-ing, trying to break our own speed records. Halfway through one pass, I jump off and spin the bison in a circle, doing a ridiculous little donut right there on the pavement. Misty hangs on like it's a tilt-a-whirl, squealing and laughing as we turn.

"I'll never forget this night!" she yells, her voice travelling out into the ether.

"Me neither," I whisper. "Me neither."

When the dizziness ends, we take a break and Misty hops off. She stands and hugs me, tightly.

I get a weird feeling this is the first time she's hugged anyone in her whole life. Or been hugged, I have no idea. But she's so warm, her body pressed against me, I don't ever want to let go.

Then, through her shirt, I feel something strange. A number of welts just like the one I saw on her arm. Raised bumps, an inch by an inch square, each one identical to the others. They're unreachably placed, a knotty cluster in the middle of her back, and as we stand there embracing it hits me and I know just what they are. Burn marks, the hot metal tip of a lighter.

Punishment.

I run my fingers up and down the scars like I'm reading bad news in Braille. After a while, she pulls away but she's not mad, not even embarrassed. I don't know what that says about her, or about me. But I think it says something.

"I'm here," I tell her. "Right here."

She smiles and pets the bison's fur. Points down the street towards the one and only convenience store in town. "Thank you for sharing your most gallant steed with me, Mr. Colin," she says. "And now in payment for this wonderful evening—if I may—the lady would like to buy the cowboy a Coke."

"THIS IS YOUR *JOB?*" Misty says as we sneak in through the back door.

I nod and resist telling her how awful it really is.

My parents run the small and tacky Wild West Museum in town and force me to work here with them so they can keep an eye on me. My *safe* uniform consists of fire retardant chaps, a dull sheriff's star and a pristine white hat, small enough so as not to obstruct my vision. They don't even let me wear real cowboy boots. These ones (which I put on at Misty's urging) have been retro-fitted with the soles of running shoes. "So you won't slip," they said, pointing out the danger of *stairs*. To top it off, they give me a brand new pair of gloves every year to protect my hands as I collect entry fees and distribute programs to customers. And no, I'm not even kidding at all.

"So do I get the big tour?" Misty asks, clapping her hands like a child.

I nod, flip on the lights, and get myself into cowboy persona.

I give her the whole spiel, switching on the museum soundtrack for effect. I show her the wax figures of Tecumseh, Pancho Villa, Jesse James. The bounty hunter room and the Sioux village, the Wild West Heroes/Villains wall, the hunting and trading display, the movie chamber with fake tumbleweeds and plastic boulders, the inevitable gift shop. Finally, when she's seen every last bit, we lie down in the Plains Room beside a replica teepee and look up at the small white lights peppering the ceiling above us. Stars.

"You're so lucky, Colin. Your parents..." Misty says.

I want to finish her sentence with, *are paranoid and can't move on.* But I stay silent, listening to the sound of the campfire crackling on the speakers.

Misty stays silent too. The lights above us, the glow of the fake moon, the random twinkling of stars. She sighs and reaches towards the sky and her sleeve slides up past her elbow. I see a mark on her arm, a small red square, swollen and puffy. It seems pretty fresh and I wonder what she could have done to herself. And why. But before I get a good look, she pulls her sleeve back down and rolls away from me. "So, so lucky," she goes on.

I reach out and very nearly touch her exposed shoulder. The warmth radiating from her soft and tender skin.

"We should get moving I suppose," she says, and I pull my hand away. We both get up, slowly, off the artificial grass.

I shut everything down and guide her towards the front door. We stop in the foyer, across from the *Welcoming Bison* that gets wheeled out each morning to entice customers inside. Misty smiles and heads over to the animal.

"Hey big fella," she says, scratching the bison's nose. "What are you doing here all by yourself? An outsider, are you?"

"Actually, they're very social animals," I say, feeling immediately stupid about being smart about bison.

"Aren't we all," she answers. And she puts her cheek right up to his, feeling the soft mane under his chin. "You could be a part of our herd," she whispers into its ear. "If we could only take you out for a walk, that is."

A walk.

I think about that for a minute. About what my parents would tell me. About the scar on Misty's arm. And then on the biggest whim of my life, I take the dog's leash and fix it around the bison's head like a set of reins. I disengage the brakes on the wheel-plate and—in my best John Wayne—say to Misty, "Hang on to that idea, little lady, and grab these here reins. 'Cause tonight is a special night. Tonight you and I, well, we can do anything we want."

I PUSH THE WINDOW OPEN while the dog sniffs after a bug in the grass. "Shhh," I tell him, as if he cares or understands. Then I lift him up, place him in the empty room, and climb in after him.

I hear the TV going at the other end of the house and I know my parents won't stray far from their seats. On this night, the anniversary, they'll be weighed down completely and as long as the dog stays quiet in the room they never enter, I'm in the clear.

It used to be mine, this room, until I was six. Back then I shared it with my little brother, Alex, for five and a half months. But that ended nine years ago. Nine years ago today.

Most of his toys still line the closet bookshelves: stuffed red dog, dinosaur mobile, the pet rock that Dad brought home, warped like Alex's head at birth; a difficult delivery they told me, but all normal in the end. In fact, everything about Alex was normal. His fingers and toes, his lungs, his heart, his eyes the colour of a pastel sky. All perfectly normal. That is, of course, until it wasn't.

I take his pillow and lift it to my face. The chalky scent of his hair, his breath like melted sugar. I bring it over to my old bed—a wooden bunk Mom and Dad abandoned immediately afterwards—and lie down with it while the dog watches from the floor. A sentinel, like I was supposed to be.

I *was* awake the night it happened, though I never admitted it. I went over to the crib, in the dark, in the quiet, and I touched Alex's forehead. I did that a lot because I wanted him to know I was there, in case he couldn't see me in the dark. I rubbed his skin, pushed back his hair, whispered, *My little brother*, and held his tiny hand. That's when I felt it. The coldness. The terrible, terrible coldness.

I put his hand down and covered him, pulling the blanket up to his stiffened chin. Then I went back to my bed and lay there, afraid to move, afraid to breathe, afraid to make any noise at all. Staring at the body through the bars of the crib until the sun rose and my parents came in and found him.

The sounds they made…

When Alex arrived I remember thinking, *From this day on, I'll never be by myself.* But then he was gone and my parents compensated by keeping me away from every*one* and every*thing*. I guess I can't blame them though, the weight of terrible things. But I'm not a baby, I'm not Alex, and I'm not afraid. I just don't want to be alone anymore.

I put the pillow back in the crib and encourage the dog to lie on the rug, scratching his belly until he's calm. I give him a treat, and another. Finally, I put the leash in one pocket, the glove in the other, and I climb back outside, quietly shutting the window behind me.

Misty's waiting in the park across the street. She doesn't ask what took so long. Instead, she takes my hand and leads me down the block. Guiding me softly, all the way to the unlit door of my parent's museum.

"WHOA THERE," I SAY. The dog's a spaniel though and doesn't care much for orders. There's dew on his belly and chest and I'll have to dry him off so my folks won't know I strayed from the *safety of the lighted streets.* I swear this dog has more fun in his life than I do. More fun by a long shot.

Up ahead, I see someone leaning against the light post,

tossing pebbles at a pop can. It's Misty from school, even from here I recognize her. The way her eyebrows rule her face, the smile that wants to come out but never does. I'm about to walk the other way when she sees me and—out of character for her—she waves. Out of character for me, I wave back.

"Hello," I approach. Misty nods, but stays quiet.

To break the silence I continue with, "It's nice to see you here. Outside of school, I mean." Stupidly, I hold out my hand to shake hers. It gets worse when I realize I'm still wearing the ridiculous glove. I slip it off and try to hide it behind my back but it falls to the ground; the dog pounces on it immediately.

Misty grins. It's a small grin, but it's there. "You're a little weird, aren't you?" she says.

I look away, thinking, *So this is what I get for taking a chance.*

But she goes on. "Oh, it's okay. Because I'm weird too, and right now I could use a bit of weirdness. The good kind."

Before I can even think about what that means, I blurt out, "Well, have you ever been to the Wild West Museum?" It's literally all I can come up with.

"Can you actually get us in there?" Misty says. The electricity in the air all around her.

"Sure. Why not?"

"Colin and Misty riding off to the Wild West—perfect!" she says.

And then she says something else but I miss it because I'm busy wrestling the glove back from the dog. It sounded like, *We're partners,* but I don't want to ask, still dazed by this whole encounter. It doesn't matter though, the thing she said, because it feels like tonight could actually turn into a good run, and a good run is much better than a bad stand. Tonight, (after I drop off the dog of course), my life might truly begin.

"Be careful," Mom says, handing me the leash. "And stick to the usual route. You don't want to upset the pup or bump into anything peculiar. Promise?"

I grunt and clip the leash to Jasper's collar.

"*Promise?*"

"Yes. I promise."

"And don't forget to wear your glove, son," Dad adds, pointing to the palm of his hand. "Leash-burn."

I sigh and put on the glove. Before I make my escape, they both storm over like I just announced I'm heading off to fight in a revolution. Mom hugs me and I can almost hear the springs creaking on the floodgate.

"Don't worry. I'll be fine," I say. "It's not like I'm *alone*." I pat the dog's head as demonstration.

Alone. Bad choice of words.

Mom starts crying and Dad turns away.

"Maybe you shouldn't… I don't know. Not tonight anyway," Mom tells me. I clench my fist inside the glove, testing the resilience of the material. I know my parents want me to kiss their cheeks right now, touch their arms, join them in a hug of eternal sadness. But I can't do it. I just can't.

"Wait a minute," Dad says. He whispers something in Mom's ear, nods in my direction, and whispers again. They face me and try to smile normally.

"Go on, son. Have fun," Dad tells me, as though letting me walk the dog is the biggest deal on earth. I'm about to say something to that effect when I realize that maybe for them, maybe tonight, it is.

"Thank you," I say. And I *do* touch their arms. Lightly, just for a second.

"Be careful though," they yell as the dog sprints forward, dragging me down the stairs. He pulls hard, towing me with the leash as we race down the drive towards the horizon ahead. The shock of cold air, the scent of possibility, the sun disappearing behind the dark, dark mountains.

"Please," they go on as I round the corner. "Just promise you'll be careful."

THE WINTER HAD BEEN LONG and the herd's strayed deep in search of food. The land here, unfamiliar to them, curious and poorly sheltered. And in the night, the wolves return for another calf.

They advance from everywhere, biting at the fringes while the herd changes direction, again and again. The cows bump into each other as they run, bashing their legs, thundering their bodies, trying to keep the calves in the centre. But they are weakened, half-starved, divided. And although the snow's retreated on the plains, the frozen ground beneath them pounds at their tired knees. One cow, a mature bison, clips a boulder and slides on the earth, scrambling. The wolves ignore it though—they aren't after an animal so big—and it clambers up again, joins the herd in the camouflage of numbers and motion. But it's only a matter of time in a struggle like this. Time, patience, precision. And they are one less.

A young bull, not yet old enough to tend a female, runs east in the attack and enters the river. Disoriented, it paddles against the flow, the air hissing from its nostrils as it swims. The water's cold and fast, full of run-off branches that tangle and churn away. The exertion as it fights the current.

Halfway across, the bison hears a wolf howling at the river's edge behind it. It swims faster, eyes bulging. On the far side it twists a hoof, splitting the hard sole as it crunches through the icy crest of the riverbank. The slippery rocks, the gut panic. The rest of the herd, heading west.

The pack leader calls out and the wolf, for the time being, retreats.

The bison continues on in the dark by scent and instinct until morning. Although it's early in the year, the rising sun feels strong; it warms the bison's back, the water steaming up as the birds stir in the distant shrub grass. It shakes—more of a forced shudder—and pain bolts through its leg, quick and unforgiving as fire. So it rests a while longer. Finally, nature and desperation overcome the hurt and the young bison starts walking. Something tells it this is what it must do. Something tells it to survive.

It eats only a small amount of sedge and grass as it trudges on. After each bite, it lifts its head and listens, inhaling deeply, searching for the scent of the herd, for a rumbling in the soil beneath its hooves. But except for a few meadowlarks and a resting family of poorwill, the bison paces alone.

When it was a calf, mere buttons in place of horns, its mother showed it things: how to cool itself with dirt; how to quell the itch of insects; how far it could stray, alone, or with its siblings in play. One night when the sun was almost down and the herd about to bed, its mother exposed an old wolf-kill, a calf from another herd. The oily scent of open bones, the dried and brittle teeth, the blood-stained earth. Death.

For this and other reasons, it longs for its mother now. For the union and company of the group.

By midafternoon, exhaustion sets in and the bison finds an old wallow dug into the ground along the trail. It circles the depression, sniffs the hardened earth, and hobbles into the bed to sleep.

Almost immediately the bison dreams. And there are no wolves in the dream. No wolves at all.

Later, when the bison wakes, it only takes a breath to realize it's still alone. And it needs to move on.

The bison's hoof aches as it steps out of the wallow. It raises that foot in rest, stands and listens for activity. But there's no danger now, no herd either; the plains, silent and bare as a bleached skull. So it moves in a circle, searching, walking slowly, keeping the weight on the other three legs. Its breath, fierce with very little exertion. Its wound, burning.

The bison knows it will have to cross that river again and the swim will prove difficult, knows the others will have travelled far while it rested. Knows that somewhere, *everywhere*, there will be wolves. Even so, it turns towards the evening sun. And after a very deep and very slow breath, carries on into the remaining light.

ACKNOWLEDGEMENTS

Versions of these stories appeared in: *The Fiddlehead; PRISM international; Grain; The Dalhousie Review; Event; Beloit Fiction Journal;* and *Coming Attractions 12*. I thank the editors of these fine publications for their support.

I am indebted to the dynamic power-pack of Matt Bowes and Claire Kelly, and to Paul Matwychuk, Kate Hargreaves and everyone at NeWest Press for trusting in this book and crafting it into being. Additional thanks to my editor, the effervescent and ever-honest Nicole Markotić, whose critical eye is as sharp as it is kind.

Many thanks to Mark Anthony Jarman for his indelible faith, being the first to believe in these stories; I owe him a cold one. To Zsuzsi Gartner for the Tlell Fall Fair conversation that turned a manuscript into a book and a lucky meeting into friendship; I owe her as well. And to Julie Paul and Sarah Selecky for excellence in path-pointing in the early days, in living rooms and coffee shops, on candled staircases, and beyond.

A group of immeasurably talented people deserve special mention: Matthew Miller, Caite Dheere, David Stewart, Holly Romanow, Frankie Blake, Danielle Janess, Barbara Campbell, Shelley Turner, Noah and Anouk. They are generous and wise scaffolders, and without their friendship this book wouldn't exist. I hold each of them close to my heart. Extra thanks to Caite for her breathtaking, collaborative artwork: one encaustic painting for each story in this collection. I am honoured.

A deep well of appreciation to Stephanie Jeffries for teaching me how to literarily run a marathon; to Dave "Monster" Hornsey for the socks (both pairs) and the stranger-than-fiction inspiration; and to Rod Deacon, the best of friends, for everything else. Wherever you are, Rod, I know you are the biggest champion, a constant guardian, and the most excellent wisecracker in the joint. We miss you.

I also owe a great deal to: Ron, Julie, Clark, Marg, Elaine, Keith, Zander, Hannah, Matt, Meesh, Sam, James, and Tim. I could not engineer a more supportive family if I tried. Thank you to my amazing children, Kenzie and Marlon, for being the inspiration in my life, the reason I strive to do more, and for withstanding extensive ridiculousness at the keyboard. They make me proud, every day, in ways I cannot measure.

And finally, I am eternally grateful to my astonishing and beautiful wife, Maria "Manasweetie" Wilkie. Hers were the first and last eyes on everything in this book and her spontaneous wit, journalistic instinct, and scope of knowledge make me appear much wiser than I actually am. Her strength is a bonfire for everyone around her, especially me. She is the love of my life. She takes me weird ways.

KEVIN A. COUTURE grew up in a BC mining town and has spent the last decade waking before dawn to write. The stories in his debut collection have all appeared in Canadian or American journals. In recent years, he has been nominated for the Writers' Trust of Canada/McClelland & Stewart Journey Prize, and was included in the anthology, *Coming Attractions*. He lives on Vancouver Island with his wife, two children, and their Brittany spaniel, who spectacularly defies animal training.